D1610506

Mad Dog

J. R. Park

Other books by J. R. Park:

TERROR BYTE
PUNCH
UPON WAKING
THE EXCHANGE
DEATH DREAMS IN A WHOREHOUSE

POSTAL with Matt Shaw
THE OFFERING: AN INTRODUCTION TO THE
SINISTER HORROR COMPANY with Daniel Marc Chant

*Visit JRPark.co.uk and SinisterHorrorCompany.com for further
information on these and other coming titles.*

J.R.PARK

SINISTER
HORROR
COMPANY

Mad Dog

First Published in 2017

Copyright © 2017 J. R. Park

Cover art and design by Vincent Hunt.
www.jesterdiablo.blogspot.co.uk
Twitter: @jesterdiablo

ISBN-13: 978-1-9997418-4-6

JRPark.co.uk

ACKNOWLEDGEMENTS

I thank these fantastic people with almost every book, each time their comments and opinions are so valuable to me that I will always be eternally grateful for their input: Thank you to Stuart Park and Steph Clitheroe for reading early versions of this book and encouraging me to keep shaping it the way it was in my head.

Also thank you to Lydian Faust for reading the final version and confirming that it wasn't a total mess.

Huge thanks to Vincent Hunt who provided the wonderful cover. The art actually came first, and it was from this design that the initial concept of the book was born.

This story would be nothing without the inspiration and encouragement from Jason Lee. Jason read Terror Byte and enjoyed it. He then eagerly provided feedback on Mad Dog's first chapter and gave me inspiration for many of the scenes that followed afterwards.

I also have to thank Daryl Duncan for providing me with some technical knowledge that I needed in the book (no spoilers here).

Finally, thanks to Duncan P Bradshaw and Daniel Marc Chant whose passion for me to finish this project never kept it far from my sights.

For Vince. This story wouldn't have existed without you.

"All stories are about wolves. All worth repeating, that is. Anything else is sentimental drivel."

      – Margaret Atwood, *The Blind Assassin*.

Darkdale prison was subject to a second serious incident in as many months. In order to understand the events that took place a series of interviews were conducted. What follows is the compiled testimonies of witnesses to this second atrocity.

ONE

Hannah Miller (University Student): You know I wasn't there, right? I had no intention of visiting, even before that bastard Mooney was in prison. Sure, you could say I *met* Mooney. *Encountered him*, would be more appropriate. *Mad Dog*, they called him, right? Jimmy told me that.

Have you ever seen him? In the flesh I mean. Everyone saw the mugshot in the newspapers. Ugly son of a bitch wasn't he? That scar running down his forehead and over his eye socket. His right eye all cloudy, grey and fucked up. God knows why he didn't get an eye patch, or get it removed and replaced with a glass one. That's what I did. You might think he looked scary in those photos, but that's nothing compared to seeing the man for real. They say there's a monster inside all of us. With Mooney, that monster was well and truly out.

I guess that's why you're talking to me. Want to know what it was like to meet the legend before he was taken to Darkdale? A bit of background for your story.

I hadn't been at University very long, still in Fresher's fortnight. Two weeks of drinking may be hard on the liver but I didn't feel it. I don't really get hangovers and all that going out was good; it had gotten me relaxed to my new surroundings very quickly.

The fortnight was coming to a close and we were all going on another fancy dress pub crawl. You wouldn't believe the amount of money I spent on costumes. This time round it was characters from kid's books and TV shows, and I went for the classic Little Red Riding Hood. Thought it would be fun. Red hooded shawl, shocking red nails, lipstick to match, short skirt, stockings. You know the look. Even bought a basket that I carried round with the mask of a wolf in it. I filled the mask with newspaper to give it bulk. Make it look like I cut the monster's head off. After a few pubs the basket and mask disappeared. No idea where I left them. But better to lose them than my purse. I've done that a few times now.

So the night is going well. Ally and Rach are on it, and I'm matching them drink for drink, shot for shot. The boys came sniffing round as usual, peacocking with all that alpha male bullshit, but we weren't interested. We were on a mission to reach oblivion and then dance our asses off until the sun came up. Fuck those Rugby boys. They make my skin crawl with their own self-importance. Never impressed me and never will.

Sorry. I'm getting side tracked.

So the basket's long gone and the drinks are flying down our throats. As I order a round of Jager bombs I'm told the card machine has stopped working. Fine time for that to happen. And although I still have my purse on me, there's no money in it. Stumbling out of the Huntsman I head to the nearest cashpoint. Surprise, surprise the thing's empty. Everyone else has beaten me to it. So I mash the keypad in frustration and head down the street looking for another one.

Now, I know I said I was comfortable with my new surroundings, but that didn't mean I knew them all too well; especially with a bloodstream rapidly filling with alcohol. I really couldn't tell you how I ended up where I did, clearly I took a wrong turning somewhere, but before I know it I'm in a deserted side street, wandering down an alley with my hand on the wall to keep myself upright. The silence is making my ears ring and the streetlights have all disappeared. Thunder rumbles somewhere off in the distance, just like in some crappy horror movie, and I start looking around, trying to get my bearings. I never knew it could get so dark in a city.

Suddenly my mind sharpens. I realise my situation. I'm lost and I'm alone. Pulling out my phone from my bag I go to call Rach when the sound of something awful echoes down the alley.

If I sounded a little blasé when I started this story, that's because I've told it so many times. After a while it becomes nothing but words. I've tried my best to divorce all feeling from them. But let me tell you, right here, right now, whatever that sound was scared the living shit out of me.

I jumped and my heart beat so hard I thought I was going to keel over. I watched the light of my phone as it fell to the floor and skated across the ground. It stopped abruptly as it careered into something big and solid. The bluish glow was faint but effective enough, and slowly my eyes made sense of the shapes it was illuminating.

At first I saw the outline of a face. The contours of a cheek and nose nearly touching the ground. It was small, child-like. A little girl, crawling in the dark. Long hair splayed out from two pigtails on her head. Her blonde bunches were filthy; muddied from soaking up what I thought was dirty puddle water. I couldn't have been more wrong.

She hadn't seen me. Probably blinded by the light of my phone.

I watched as she stretched out her hands, gripped the ground and pulled herself along, dragging her belly over the concrete. She was shivering and I went to call out; to ask if she was alright, but that noise came again and took my voice. A dog-like growl.

Like a frightened deer, my instincts told me to freeze.

A patter of footsteps, like bare feet running across concrete, caught my ears.

The girl rolled onto her back. The light of my phone fully illuminated her face, and I can see these awful slashes across her cheeks, drenching her in blood. Flaps of torn skin dangle from her face. It was just horrible. Her eyes were like saucers, wide with terror as she stared back into the black.

Another growl echoed round the alley, only this time much louder.

Much closer.

The girl must have seen something and tried to scream, but fainted before she could make a sound, her head hitting the concrete with a sickening thud. A dark puddle of what must have been blood oozed from her cracked skull and I watched, stunned, as her body gently rocked from the influence of something else. Someone hidden in the dark.

Holding my breath, I tried to focus on the darkness, to peer through the night. Eventually my perseverance paid off. Slowly I made out a large figure, squatted and hunched over the poor, unconscious girl. At first I thought he was wearing a fur coat, but as I saw his muscles flex underneath, I realised it wasn't a coat at all. He was completely naked.

This was how I met *Mitch Mad Dog Mooney*.

I didn't know it was him of course, back then he wasn't the notorious figure he is now.

His hands were huge, ending in points, like claws that gripped hold of the poor girl. His ears seemed to rise above his hair, and his eyes; his eyes glowed in the dark, reflecting the light from my phone like a cat caught in headlights.

But it's when I traced the sounds of grunts and tearing, when I saw his mouth, that I felt my legs nearly collapse from under me. Maybe it was a mixture of the shadows and alcohol, but his jaw looked like it was pulled out of shape, into a weird, elongated snout. I know, crazy right? But the first thing I thought of when I saw him was the mask I'd stuffed with newspaper and lost with my basket.

He opened his mouth and exposed a set of over-sized teeth. I winced as I watched him sink them into the flesh of that little girl. Her ribs snapped as he bit down, and as he tore apart her chest, I watched those broken ribs drop to the floor. I wanted to run, my brain screamed at me to get out of there, but like a bad bout of sleep paralysis, my body refused to listen. He took another bite, this time into the soft flesh of her stomach. My own belly stirred in disgust, but I couldn't take my eyes off the trails of gristle and skin that hung from his chin, dripping in blood.

It was only when he stopped chewing those monstrous jaws and his eyes looked up into mine did the spell slowly begin to subside. Those eyes glowed with a bright intensity, and even then I noticed the difference in his right eye. It was a subtle shade darker.

My foot edged back slowly away from him, but I kept him squarely in my vision. He rose from his crouching position and I watched as he towered above me.

And then the little girl turned her head.

She looked at me, her face all twisted and weak like my Grandmother's before she died. Tears glistened in her eyes and blood poured from her mouth as she wrestled with her words. It was low and very faint, like a whisper. But I heard it clear enough. A warning from someone that had already accepted their death.

'Go away!'

I wasn't about to argue. I had no choice. My cover had been blown. I was no longer the scared deer, I was the hunted rabbit. I turned and ran, but he was on me too quickly. I felt him catch hold of my cape and pull me backwards. Stupid costume! I landed on my ass but rolled away, instinct and adrenaline propelling me forward. Climbing back to my feet I tried to sprint off, but was swiped in the side by one of those awful claws. A pain shot up my body as I fell forward, crashing into a wheelie bin. It knocked the wind from me as I slumped to my knees, dazed and clutching at my side.

I didn't look up to see him stood over me; *I could sense it.*

I could feel the warmth of his hunger, the evil in those eyes.

The sound of his panting grew louder as he bent down to look at me. The fucker knew he had me trapped. His breath was warm against my cheek, but I refused to look. I couldn't accept this nightmare. I wouldn't allow it in.

I swear I could feel his teeth on my skin.

And then I lashed out. With my clutch bag still in my hand, I swung at his head, hoping maybe I'll get a shot at that dodgy eye. Not a hope in hell! It was like lighting the touch paper. All of a sudden he launched at me. I looked up to see those glowing eyes, the snapping of those terrible teeth; the ripping claws that reached out for me.

I turned and clung to the wall, trying to pull myself up and get away, but he knocked me to the floor and was on top of me with a strength I couldn't hope to fight.

Everything went red as he snapped and clawed. I held my hands up, pushing at his face to fend him off, but he just kept coming. Blood poured down my fingers, making them indistinguishable from the nail-varnished tips I'd so lovingly painted hours earlier. Had he bitten them off? I couldn't tell. Obvious now, huh?

The pain going through my body was so immense, so overwhelming, that I just stopped feeling it. Every strike to my face, every bite towards my head left a washed out stinging sensation, muted with shock.

I'm not sure if I remember the next part, or my brain

filled in the blanks with its own story, as when I recall it, it's like I'm watching it from afar. Like I'm watching it on a movie.

My arms won't move, I'm exhausted and blood is pouring down me. He grabs my throat and picks me up; lifts me so we're at eye-level, my feet dangling uselessly in mid-air. I'm done fighting and I watch as he pulls his other arm back like he's ready to swing at me; tear my face off with that huge claw. His lips curl up like an angry dog, exposing his teeth that are now dripping in *my* blood.

This is it then, Little Red Riding Hood, I remember thinking to myself as I finally gave in.

I close my eyes tight. The stinging and injuries make my face feel strange.

Like a mask.

The next thing I know, I hear a voice.

'Over there!' a man called out. 'Put the girl down.'

All of a sudden there's a strange sound and I'm gritting my teeth as my whole body tightens and a new type of pain courses through me. I feel Mooney let go and I fall to the floor; the pain dissipating as quickly as it came.

I roll over and understand what's happened. I watch as more tasers are fired at him. The electrodes dig into his body. He struggles with them for a moment, trying to pull them from his skin as he staggers towards the police, but eventually he drops. I'm trying to stay awake, elated I'm alive, but the shock is all too much for me. As I fight unconsciousness I look over to the fallen Mooney. The monster does indeed look bestial, but as I begin to accept my safety he appears more human.

They say fear makes the wolf grow bigger. Well it works in reverse too. Security makes the monster more tragic.

My sympathies reach out to my attacker and I can't stop smiling as I look at the unconscious man next to me. I hear the police kneel by my side, but their words are a blur. I look at Mooney's scarred and beaten face and I see a pained peace in his slow breaths.

Tears rolls down my cheeks, only they're not tears. I understand this when I go to brush them away. As I wipe my eye I feel something long and thin poking into it. But it's not going *in*, it's coming *out*. My fingers feel around the edge of the eye socket, itself nothing more than the rim to a hole in my face. I follow the fleshy cord that hangs out of my skull, scooping up the organic twine in my hand until I come to a dead, fleshy orb at the end. *My eye.*

Sympathy turns to anger, but *his* expression remains the same.

As I looked on, I hoped he'd die that night.

A part of me thinks he did too.

J. R. Park

TWO

J. R. Park

Jimmy Eades (Prisoner): Have you ever seen the moon, far away from the man-made glow of cities and towns? It's beautiful. It lights up the countryside. Turns the whole place into a ghost world. Shadows move that shouldn't in that light.

From the notes of Dr Edwards (Prison Doctor): A considerable number of studies have been conducted in the correlation between specific stages of the lunar cycle and behaviour in humans. Despite popular belief that the full moon influences our moods, none of these studies have been able to satisfactorily demonstrate the existence of a so called *lunar effect*.

Jimmy Eades: I used to go lamping back when I was a kid and lived in the country. Waiting in the dark for the rabbits to come out. Watching their silvery silhouettes move in the moonlight. Quietly you'd watch them, then when one of them got close enough you'd shine a torch directly at it. The little bugger would stop still, dazzled by the bright light, unable to move.

You only had seconds, so you had to be quick, but whilst your friend has that bunny startled in the beam, you've got to run round the side, grab it from the neck if you can, and plunge your knife in deep.

The more practice you get, the cleaner kill. The first few times you catch one you're covered, absolutely covered, in blood. Might even fumble and let the blighter accidentally escape. Poor little thing, trying to crawl off with a leg sliced open, its guts trailing behind it, or a hole in its throat that's pissing blood all over the place and an eye lost to the point of your blade.

Anything in that state's not going to get very far. It's easy to hunt down. Put it out of its misery. But that's not the way to kill something. Prolonged suffering should be saved for your enemies. And whoever had a beef with a rabbit?

From the notes of Dr Edwards: Despite the lack of evidence, the common belief of a lunar effect is still widely held, even in modern societies where most folklore has either been discredited or forgotten. Police officers and hospital workers are often quoted, regularly experiencing their busiest periods during the phase of a full moon.

Jimmy Eades: Prolonged suffering. The poor rabbits with their back legs buckled and snapped, waiting for death. That's what I thought of when I first entered Darkdale. The other prisoners looked shocked, haunted by something. I could see the ghosts of something awful in their eyes. Of course I found out what, later on. But it wasn't public knowledge at the time. The powers that be were doing their best to keep a lid on exactly what happened. But the truth came out didn't it? The truth always comes out. Eventually.

But you're not here to talk about that. Not if you're talking to me. You want to know about the final nail in Darkdale's coffin. You want to know about Mitch *Mad Dog* Mooney.

Peter Ball (Prison Guard): There wasn't really a trial. Not a proper one. They wanted him safely behind bars as fast as they could. The media had whipped their readers up into a fury of disgust. They didn't care to question just what goes on inside a man's head to make him do such things. *I mean eating a girl!* He was a monster. The newspapers and public demanded he be sent to the harshest, meanest prison we had.

The Prime Minister was happy to oblige. Earnt him some much needed brownie points, and what with the elections only round the corner… You know how these things go.

From the notes of Dr Edwards: Despite the lack of substantial evidence, research does suggest tantalising possibilities. In 1978 the Journal of Clinical Psychiatry published the results of data analysed to determine whether a relationship exists between the lunar synodic cycle and human aggression. To quote from the abstract published on PubMed.gov: *Homicides, suicides, fatal traffic accidents, aggravated assaults and psychiatric emergency room visits occurring in Dade County, Florida all show lunar periodicities.*

Homicides and aggravated assaults demonstrate statistically significant clustering of cases around a full moon.

Peter Ball: The prisoners had been through a lot already. Darkdale was still recovering; being repaired from the time before. The North Tower was being held up by scaffolding, being fixed and out of bounds. That put pressure on the accommodation. Suddenly we'd lost a good twenty cells, and whilst the prisoners had all been like docile cattle in the first few weeks following it all, it was never going to last.

The news of this *Mad Dog's* impending arrival understandably stirred a wave of unrest that grew bigger the longer it reverberated.

I think we all tried to ignore it. Pretend it wasn't there. After all, lightning doesn't strike in the same place twice. At least, that's what we told ourselves.

Jimmy Eades: I always wanted to be a writer. Outside of prison I had a notebook with me at all times, scribbling ideas or capturing experiences so as not to lose them. I wasn't allowed one in Darkdale, not until I'd earned the privilege, and even then I couldn't take it from the library. But that didn't matter. My first few weeks in that hellhole have been imprinted on my brain. I remember it like it was yesterday.

I used to stay up at night, watching the moon shine through the bars, lighting up my cell. There was no way I could sleep. I wanted to cry, but didn't want to show weakness. Not in front of my cellmate, Forbes. I shouldn't have been here. I was terrified. This was all a mistake.

Oliver Coleborn (Lawyer): It was an unfortunate turn of events. Despite the severity of Mr Eades' sentence, Darkdale was not the prison best suited for him. His placement there would appear to be the circumstance of government cutbacks and prison overcrowding.

Father Matthews (Prison Chaplain): Young Jimmy Eades was in the wrong prison. He should never have been in Darkdale. I spoke to Dr Edwards at the time, and she agreed. Of course Governor Peel didn't listen to either of us. He had no time for me. I was viewed as nothing more than a spiritual chew toy for the prisoners. As for the good doctor? Well, let's just say Governor Peel had some old fashioned views. I don't think it ever sat right with him that a female doctor had been appointed to a male prison.

From the notes of Dr Edwards: The University of Liverpool published a paper in May 2000, reporting that results showed a significant change at the time of the full moon only in subjects with a diagnosis of schizophrenia.

Jimmy Eades: Hannah wouldn't come visit me. My own girlfriend. I know she'd just started University, but still, we were in love. I was mad at first, thought she was being out of line. She's one of those beautiful but crazy girls, you know? Our relationship could get quite intense, spending so much time together. After a while she used to hide away for a few days every month. Go visit her aunt or something. I was glad of the peace. But those first few weeks in prison, I needed to see her.

Peter Ball: Mad Dog Mooney was a ghost story. A legend that spooked even the most hardened of criminals. Originally an enforcer for Hamish the Hammer, tales of his sadistic acts spread far and wide, whispered in fear between cellmates at night.

Jimmy Eades: Word got to me from my family about her attack. I didn't know about the circumstances. Not to start with. I was glad to be given time to write to her. Father Matthews said it was a useful distraction. I used to send her letters every few days, just to let her know I cared. She didn't write many back, but then it's me that wants to be the writer.

Peter Ball: Mooney is the monster that haunts the nightmares of the most sick and violent people you will ever meet.

Jimmy Eades: Maybe she was offended by my spelling. I'd never been very confident with that. As a kid I was so conscious of it I saved up my pocket money and bought a dictionary. A dictionary's a dictionary, right? Well apparently not. Even though I'd taken extra care to check my words with it, I can still remember the humiliation of my teacher berating me in front of the whole class for my careless spelling. I tried to defend myself; explain what I'd done. When I pulled out my pocket-sized dictionary to show him, Mr Heywood's eyes widened and he ripped it from my hands. My face burnt with embarrassment as he scolded me. I was only thirteen. How was I to know it was an American dictionary?

I just hoped she was okay. Hannah. An attack like that can be really harmful, not just physically, but mentally, you know?

Peter Ball: He was all kinds of messed up. And he was coming to Darkdale.

THREE

Jorge Wiles (Prisoner): The first thing anyone asks when you're in prison is: *What are you in for?* The second is: *How long you got?* On the outside when you meet someone new you might ask: *What do you do?* It's the prison version of that.

Jimmy Eades (Prisoner): I was ashamed of why I was there; I didn't like to admit it. I'm still ashamed now.

Peter Ball (Prison Guard): I know you want to get to the night in question, but it's important you understand the background; the context.

Jimmy Eades: I moved to the city the summer before her enrolment so I could be near Hannah during her study. You know, to set up a base. A nest.

I got a job working in a warehouse. It wasn't a bad job; taking deliveries, packing up shipments. It was hauling boxes and doing paperwork. I wasn't scared of hard work and the money was good. My plan was to get my forklift training complete. I was ready to go, just needed to complete the practical.

That was until I got made redundant. *Cut backs* they said. Had nothing to do with the boss's son taking a job? Yeah right.

Jorge Wiles: I first met Jimmy at the library. He looked wired, but that was Jimmy's way, like a coiled spring. Sometimes he seemed scared, nervous. Other times the opposite. But he was always hyper aware. Always alert. And almost always in the library.

Jimmy Eades: So I was *last one in, first one out.* To add insult to injury I was given no notice and no final pay. They said there was an error in the system and I'd have to wait. I called horseshit and threw a punch, angry that I was going to be turfed out of my flat if I couldn't make the rent.

I was sent packing with a black eye and a split lip.

Peter Ball: The facilities at Darkdale were tired and old before… well, you know. It wasn't just the North Tower that was out of action. We were instructed to keep an eye on power consumption and turn off all lights that weren't in use. Our connection to the grid was dodgy to say the least, a fault that was still being looked at, and we only had one emergency generator running.

Jorge Wiles: It took a while for him to open up. But as I was head of the prison library he'd see me almost every day as he came in to read books or write letters. That kid sure loved to write.

Jimmy Eades: I should have just left it there, but my mind turned over and over. Everything was fucked. As I walked out of the office, Mr Creevy called out to me, saying he'd make sure I never got work in this town again. I believed him. His businesses had made him a big player. Mr Creevy was perfectly capable of screwing me over, and the bloody nose I'd given him was the perfect reason to do so.

Peter Ball: Tensions were simmering. The prisoners were not being treated with respect. The lesson here is if you treat people badly, they're going to treat you badly back. I can't say it any more simply.

Jorge Wiles: I used to say hi, but Jimmy would just smile meekly and scurry away to his table. I guess my size does make me a bit intimidating. I certainly didn't tell him why I was banged up. He'd have run a mile.

Jimmy Eades: I couldn't think straight. I headed to the nearest pub, sat in a quiet corner and drank. I needed to turn my anger off for a moment. I thought the booze might incapacitate me; render me unconscious. But it did the opposite. It fanned the flames of my hatred; egging me on to do what I did.

Craig Creevy (Son of Mr Jonathan Creevy): That Eades kid is fucking dead. If I ever get in the same room as that shit it'll be the last five minutes of his miserable life.

Jorge Wiles: In Darkdale everyone has blood on their hands.

Jimmy Eades: Jorge didn't ask why I was in prison. I guess that's why I started talking to him. It helped to have normal conversations, divorced from the bars and guards that surrounded us. We both read, although I was more into the classics and he was a Stephen King fan. The thing we talked about the most was music. Seemed weird to have a conversation about music in a library.

Jorge Wiles: I should have known he was a Techno-head. All that energy. I can imagine him bouncing around like Tigger. I used to explain the similarities between Techno and Metal. He used to listen with an intrigued smile. I can guarantee he'll be listening to a Heart Of A Coward record the next chance he gets.

Metal is a great way of venting pent up aggression, and might have done the lad some favours. You should have seen him go mental about the dictionary we had. "What's with this American bullshit?" He just let loose one day, tearing out its pages.

Peter Ball: All it takes is one little catalyst.

Jimmy Eades: I'd just come back from speaking with my mum. She'd been to visit and told me all about Hannah's attack. She showed me the newspaper cutting of the man that did it. Nasty looking fucker. In a way I was relieved there was some explanation as to why Hannah hadn't come. But that was fleeting.

I could feel the anger stirring inside, bubbling in the pit of my stomach and swelling until it filled every part of me. My mum told me to calm down. I watched the guards smirk with an untold joke and before I know it they're leading my mother away, telling me visiting time is over.

Jorge Wiles: He marched into the library visibly twitching. I'd never seen him like this before. He launched at the dictionary and after I wrestled the remains of it from his hands, I sat him down and tried to get some level of calm; but it didn't work. We never did get the chance to talk about it.

Jimmy Eades: So I'm back in the library, Jorge has a hand on my shoulder and a look of compassion in his eye. I can feel myself well up. I want to cry. I want to tell him everything; to release it all. Then all of a sudden a noise echoes round Darkdale.

We stop talking and listen. One of the prisoners is howling.

The howl is joined by another, then another. The sound gets louder as more of the prisoners join in; banging against walls and doors to add to the din. It fills the halls, bouncing off the walls; real shrill like, and getting into my head.

The reason for the commotion becomes apparent as I hear the sound of heavy footsteps booming down the corridor. At first I see a shape, a large black hulk of a shadow through the frosted glass of the library window. Its steps are ponderous, but deliberate. I watch the shadows of the guards, puny in comparison, walk beside him, and I can feel their fear.

Running to the library entrance and looking down the hall, I want to get a better look, but I'm not prepared for what I see.

Coming towards me is the same face I saw in the newspaper. He must have been seven foot tall, and half as wide. His hair was dark and wild, turning into a short, unkempt beard halfway down his face. His scowl creased up his skin, highlighting this huge scar that ran across his forehead, over his eye socket and down his right cheek.

As he passes by he looks directly at me, his mismatched eyes, one cloudy and lifeless, stare into mine. I swallow hard and feel my legs buckle from under me. The worst possible blend of fury and terror filled my veins.

I'd just looked into the face of the devil.

Peter Ball: Mad Dog had arrived.

Jimmy Eades: You didn't need to ask him what he was in for. His expression, his scars, told their own story. Whatever atrocity you could imagine doing, he'd probably done it.

FOUR

Peter Ball (Prison Guard): A small amount of blood spread thinly over the ground can make one hell of a mess.

Jimmy Eades (Prisoner): The devil had arrived in Darkdale prison, but the place already had its own resident demons.

Peter Ball: A full blood-donation bag holds just under a pint. Split one of those open and it will cover a room. Make it look like the centre of a massacre.

Jimmy Eades: Those demons had been quiet. I'd certainly not encountered them here. But the devil must have woken them from their slumber, for that very same night three of them entered my cell.

Father Matthews (Prison Chaplain): Looking back on it, there were a lot of errors made. Silly mistakes that by themselves didn't mean a lot. But put them together and they all added up.

Jimmy Eades: These demons went by the name of the Websters. Mark, Rich and Mike. All brothers, and all doing time in the same prison.

Father Matthews: I had nothing to do with the administration side of things. But with hindsight I should have listened to my gut. I should have said something. Bad decisions were made by the management, all in the name of efficiency. Overcrowding meant people were put where they would fit. It was seen as a simple numbers game.

Jorge Wiles (Prisoner): We were all thrown in on top of each other. It didn't help to keep things calm when you have prisoners rubbing shoulders in an already claustrophobic environment. If not monitored properly the wrong people are going to meet. Incidents become inevitable.

Jimmy Eades: It was night time, everyone should have been asleep, but something woke me and I watched these three ghouls walk into my cell. The door was inexplicably open and they sauntered in like they owned the place.

The balding one, Mike, put his hand over my mouth and an index finger to his smiling lips, motioning me to be quiet. Scared out of my wits, I froze like one of the rabbits I used to hunt. I had no intention of making a sound. After a moment Mike became assured of my compliance and turned his attention to his brothers. They in turn were talking to the man in the bunk beneath mine: my cellmate, Forbes.

Jorge Wiles: Forbes was an okay guy. He was in prison, so he was a scumbag like the rest of us. But for a scumbag he was alright. I don't think he deserved what he got. We never knew *exactly* what happened to him, but the prison rumour-mill filled in the blanks.

Peter Ball: On average the human body holds around eight pints of blood. Spray that around a room and that's going to take hours to clean.

Jimmy Eades: Mark Webster crouched down next to Forbes and spoke with a sinister calmness. "It's so good we finally got to meet," he said, gently but intimidatingly running his fingers down the man's cheek. "We've heard a lot about you since we've been inside. Heard the bullshit you've been talking. Seems you've been running your mouth off about us one too many times. Seems like it got back to us, doesn't it? Got anything to say?"

Forbes went to speak, but before he could utter a word in defence, Rich launched a vicious jab, at his jaw. I heard Forbes' muffled whine below me as he held his face. I heard him spitting broken teeth from his blood-filled mouth. I heard him whimper as he failed to hide his fear.

"I didn't catch that?" Mark said; and even though I couldn't see him, I could sense the beaming smile in his tone.

Taking a moment to compose himself, Forbes

swallowed back blood before answering. He went to speak and *bang*! Once again Rich's knuckles struck his jaw before he finished the first word. Forbes howled in agony and more teeth scattered onto the tiles below.

"Are you getting it yet?" Mark asked, nodding his head to force understanding.

The pair pulled him out of his bunk and threw him to the floor. I heard his nose split as he hit the ground face first.

Rich held up an object; a long, thin piece of wood. Catching sight of the chalked end, I recognised it as one of the pool cues from the table downstairs.

A groan came from Forbes as they tore at his clothes, wrestling to hold him still as they pulled his trousers off. Morbid curiosity made me want to see, but Mike had my head held firmly on the pillow, and I didn't dare fight his grip for fear of receiving the same treatment. As Rich studied the end of the cue, I caught the flash of his twisted grin; his teeth seemed to glow in the darkness like the moon on a moorland night.

He knelt down to the floor and disappeared from my vision. I could only guess as to exactly what was happening. In a way I was thankful I couldn't see; the sounds alone brought bile to my throat.

Jorge Wiles: A wide reader has a strong imagination, and Jimmy loved his books.

Jimmy Eades: I imagined Mark clenching Forbes' butt cheeks and prising them apart whilst his brother, Rich, directed the tip of the pool cue toward the opening of the victim's anus. I squirmed in sympathy as Forbes tried to scream. His cries were muffled as Mark gagged him on his own trousers, forcing them down his throat.

The chalked tip must have penetrated into his dry rectum as those muted screams changed pitch and tears rolled down his cheeks. He thrashed about on the floor, but was unable to escape, held firm by Mark. The Websters grinned as Rich jabbed the wooden shaft, brutally driving it further and further up the poor man's ass. Forbes broke into a sob as I heard something wet tear; something internal. The cue must have ripped through his colon, tearing a hole through the lining as it was forced further into his body.

Rich pulled the cue backwards and forwards, inside and out. A wet, slapping sound filled the cell as wood punctured flesh, pushing and pushing, until there was only a handhold left exposed between the poor wretch's quivering legs.

I smelt the stench as Forbes' bowels gave up and expelled its contents, the motion of the makeshift weapon forcing out a foul stream of blood and shit that flooded the floor.

My cellmate yelped like an animal, gargling in blood, as the shaft was shoved even deeper inside his body and stirred in jerky, circular movements; twisting his internal organs into a knotted mess. His mewling grew weaker as tried to claw through the puddle of his own fluids, splashing in a filthy pool of excrement as he failed to find grip and pull himself away from his tormentors.

I can only guess at what kind of agony Forbes suffered, and what kind of damage it would have caused, but it must have punctured his lungs, twisted his intestines and finally speared his heart.

I heard his head crack against the floor with such force it caused me to shudder. His whimpering and gasps for breath had ceased. The only sound I could hear was that of bubbling liquid as blood and crap oozed from his body, hurried along by the gases that forced their exit from his lifeless corpse.

Softly, I heard Mark whisper to him. I recognised the quote instantly. It was Shakespeare. From Othello to be exact.

"Who steals my purse steals trash; 'tis something, nothing;
'Twas mine, 'tis his, and has been slave to thousands;
But he that filches from me my good name
Robs me of that which not enriches him,
And make me poor indeed."

Peter Ball: Take into account the shit, the broken teeth, and all the guts that fell out of that poor guy's ass; well you'd better have a strong stomach.

Jimmy Eades: Mike smiled at me and whispered, "You didn't see us, alright boy? This was our business. Between him and us. You stay out of it."

He kissed me softly on the cheek and gave an unhinged giggle before I watched the three leave as casually as they entered, like apparitions fading into the night.

Father Matthews: He was found crying in his bed. The guards were pretty brutal in Darkdale. Forcing him to clean up that cell was out of line.

Peter Ball: Someone had to do it. It certainly wasn't

going to be me.

Jimmy Eades: It took me most of the night to mop up the mess. The smell alone made me puke in my own bucket. The guards stood around and watched, baying and jeering as I slipped on Forbes' guts and wretched at having to scoop up his shit with my own bare hands. This was clearly what passed as their entertainment.

Father Matthews: You had to wonder sometimes, just who was worse? Or was it neither? Are we all monsters deep down? Does the devil lurk inside us all?

Jorge Wiles: We all do bad things.

Jimmy Eades: Now I understood, I was truly in hell with demons on all sides. I was glad when I was allowed to go back to sleep, thankful the smell of bleach covered up the stench that still clung to my fingers.

As grateful as I was for the rest, even the usual comfort of the coming daylight did nothing but bring the threat of another monster; this one, however, wore a suit and tie.

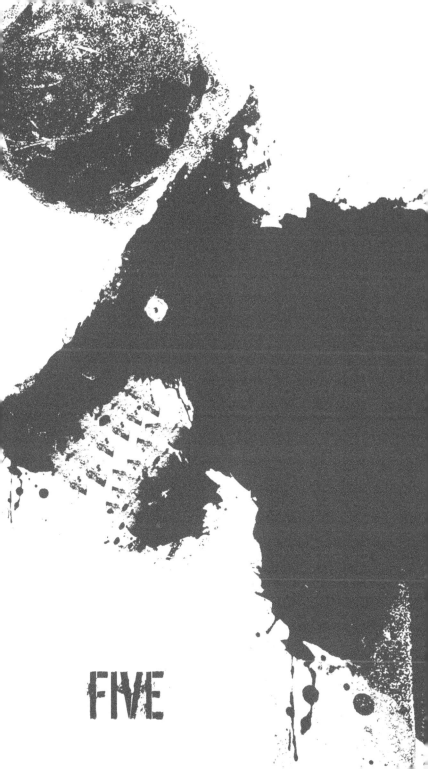

FIVE

Jorge Wiles (Prisoner): Mr Peel, the Governor, held no pretension about what he was. He was a monster, through and through, and he was proud of it. The tough bastard worked hard on keeping that reputation.

Peter Ball (Prison Officer): The prisoners easily outnumber the staff of any prison you'd care to think of. The prison system as a whole has been reported as being overcrowded every year since 1994. With Darkdale it was worse than most. Staff shortages and a prison reaching bursting point meant that at the lowest point on the staff rota, usually an hour before the nightshift took over, when the part timers had left and what remained of the day staff held the fort, we were down to a ratio of one guard per ten prisoners. Sometimes even less.

With numbers like that you can be overrun at any moment. So you rule the roost either with trust or fear. And our Governor was not a trusting man.

Jimmy Eades (Prisoner): I knew what was coming, I'd met Governor Peel on my induction. He was just the same then as he was during this grilling. He knew I'd never say anything. A grass isn't going to live long in prison, especially in Darkdale. So I guess, in a way he took it in good humour.

"Maybe you'd like to spend the night in a cell with our newest resident?" he threatened. Of course he meant Mooney, but that didn't shake me. I knew he was bluffing.

"You'll be dead by the morning!"

This was probably true, but I could sense there was no intent behind his bluster.

"You aren't making any friends here, Eades!" he bellowed. I could smell his breakfast on his breath. Boiled eggs. I felt myself go green. "The lads tell me you did a pretty sloppy job of cleaning up that mess last night. I think you need the practice. From now on you'll be assigned to the cleaning team."

I clenched my stomach as I thought back to last night, trying to stop it from gurgling. The dry retch caught me completely by surprise. The jet of vomit was a total shock.

I was hypnotised by the splatter of puke that coated his desk. I straightened up, but kept my head lowered. I dared not look at his face.

"You'll do the floors and showers," he continued, taking in my transgression and growing madder. "The shit-caked toilets too. Every single one of them. You'll learn how to do it properly. Understood?"

I stared, transfixed by the puddle of bile. From my

peripheral vision I could see the Governor's face turning red as he leaned over his desk towards me. "And you can start with this goddamn mess."

The louder he shouted the more he hoped others saw him being a badass.

Peter Ball: Even then the Governor was growing concerned. He spoke to me after the adjudication with Eades and was worried we'd be lurching from one catastrophe to the next. He ordered a full investigation into the death of Forbes. The whole prison knew what had happened, but this needed to be handled through official channels.

Jimmy Eades: The adjudication went better than I'd expected. I think he must have taken pity on me. Maybe because I looked so tired and scared, which wasn't an act.

I was given my own cell for the time being and the guards kept an eye on me just to make sure I was going to be alright. Once the Websters realised I wasn't a grass I figured I'd be okay.

After I'd wiped down and disinfected his desk I thought that would be it for the day, but I got drafted back into my cleaning job earlier than expected.

Jorge Wiles: I guess you guys don't know much about prison life. The walls are grey, the lights are harsh and CCTV follows you. Doesn't sound much different to the outside, does it? Trouble, however, is handled much more effectively in her majesty's hotel. The moment trouble starts up, one of the guards rings a bell. That bell is a signal for all the other guards to come running in after them. Then it's all clubs and boots until the troublemakers are pulverised to the ground, bleeding and spitting out teeth.

All phones were banned from Darkdale. That way there's no one taking a video to sue their asses in a court case.

Peter Ball: Our methods may not be approved by the outside world, but you've got to remember, this is the scum of society altogether under one roof. We respond in a way they'll understand.

Jimmy Eades: It's all part of the induction. The meet and greet of Darkdale.

Jorge Wiles: We've all had the warning. *"You hear the sound of a buzzer? That means there's trouble. Don't go running over to have a gawp. We're dealing with it and if you get in the way you become part of that trouble. Understood?"*

Jimmy Eades: No one takes any notice. If there's a piece of action going on, of course we want to take a look. Anything to break up the monotony. Which is why I couldn't help but follow the guards when they ran past me, responding to that ear splitting alarm.

By the time I'd got there they'd surrounded Mooney in the canteen. His top was black with blood and the floor around him shone almost pink under the fluorescent lights. He wiped the gore from his mouth with his sleeve and dropped the broken body in his hand. The prisoner fell to the floor, but they didn't make a sound. They were already unconscious. Their head rolled on their neck and rested face up, eyes closed and their mouth open; blood smeared across their features.

"He started it," Mooney growled in a low, booming voice. "I finished it."

I looked through the crowd of nervous guards and recognised the unconscious prisoner. The last time I saw him, that gaping mouth, it had been used to plant a condescending kiss on my cheek. That was Mike Webster!

Jorge Wiles: Every community has a pecking order. Someone else comes in and the big birds are going to peck at him, try to assert dominance. I suppose someone had to have a go. More fool them.

Jimmy Eades: Turns out Mike had walked up to him whilst they were all sat down eating lunch. Started giving it the big talk. Telling him how the Websters ran Darkdale, how Mad Dog was nothing round here, how Hamish the Hammer was dead and Carlito John couldn't save his sorry ass in *their* territory.

I don't think he expected to receive quite the maddening response he provoked.

Looking at the patches of blood on the walls, dripping from impact craters in the plaster at head height, I'd say Mike Webster had been made very clear who was the nothing round here. By the angle of Mike's legs and the weird bends in his fingers, I'd say Mad Dog made a point of underlining that fact.

Peter Ball: Guys like that are the reason we carry

weapons.

Jimmy Eades: The Governor came storming through. "What the hell is going on here?!" he bellowed across a stunned room. "Guards, escort that menace back to his cell, from now on he's in solitary. Mooney, so help me you'd better co-operate, or you'll be crying pepper spray for weeks. Someone get that poor bastard to the Doctor," he pointed at the broken body of Mike Webster. "As for the rest of you," he said, looking at the gathered crowd, "this place is on lockdown until I say so. Everyone get back to your cells."

I went to leave, but the Governor collared me. "Where are you going Eades? You're the cleaner. Clean this fucking mess up."

Jorge Wiles: Governor Peel screamed and shouted, giving it a good show of being in charge, but he kept well clear; always keeping a line of guards in front of him.

Jimmy Eades: The Governor was a monster and proud of it. But Mooney was the nightmare even the monsters feared.

SIX

From the notes of Dr Edwards (Prison Doctor): I was shocked and dismayed to see James Eades forced into cleaning duties. I have yet to be given a full report on the incident in his cell the night before, as it's still pending a full investigation, but from what little I know I have advised against this kind of treatment. To say the ways of Governor Peel and his staff are foolhardy and barbaric would be an understatement.

Jimmy Eades (Prisoner): It was eerie, being all alone in that canteen, mopping up Mike Webster's blood from the cracked tile flooring. A guard stood outside, waiting for me to finish, but aside from the faint click as he cracked his tattooed knuckles, the prison was deathly silent.

I'd never been anywhere other than in my cell during a lockdown before.

I gagged less this time at the splattered mess on the ground. Maybe I was getting used to this kind of thing, or maybe it was because I thought Mike Webster deserved everything he got. I found myself smiling as I thought back to the retribution he'd been dished out. Mad Dog Mooney had unwittingly become my avenging angel. Don't get me wrong, I held no sympathy for him either. He'd attacked Hannah. Scarred her. For that there was no forgiveness.

I hated him like nothing else.

I gripped the mop handle in anger, feeling my knuckles grow tight against the skin as I thought about what he'd done to her.

Trying to calm myself and stop for a moment, I listen to the wind ripping through the abandoned North Tower. It was boarded up, waiting for the builders to do their best to salvage it. But the wind blew through gaps in the broken windows, hitting the makeshift steel doors that were padlocked closed, keeping everyone out. The locks rattled and the hinges creaked on their brackets. The autumn gales howled like the moans of condemned souls. Fitting I thought.

Wheeling my bucket full of red water out of the canteen, I stopped in the main hallway for a moment and looked up, enjoying the enforced serenity that had briefly taken Darkdale. I could see all the way to the top, all three storey's with their walkways round the side. A chain-linked mesh blanketed the drop over the edge of the railings on each storey. I guess it was there to stop suicides, or people throwing others off. I hadn't given it much thought until then, but as I watched them gently sway, glistening from the harsh lights that shone from the ceiling, sprayed by the trickle of water that dripped from small leaks in the weather-worn roof, I smiled. Like metallic webs, I mused taking in the beauty of something I'd never appreciated before.

I closed my eyes, swept up in this majesty of the mundane, and for a moment I imagined the refreshing feel of rain on my face. I imagined it washing my soul as it washed my skin, freeing me from all the things I'd done wrong over the years.

In that moment I found peace. My thoughts were silenced. There was nothing but calm.

Peter Ball (Prison Guard): The place had never been so quiet. I think everybody was stunned. The incident in the North Tower continued to haunt us, and what with the last two outbreaks of violence in such short succession, bang, everybody needed to get some rest. I think we were *all* in shock.

Jimmy Eades: My tranquillity was fleeting, quickly broken by the calling of my name. The guards had another job for me and led me, mop in hand, towards the end of the wing.

From the notes of Dr Edwards: It took a fracas in the canteen today, but Governor Peel has finally come round to my way of thinking.

Jimmy Eades: They unbolted a heavy set door. I thought it unusual; the rest of the doors, cells included, worked on electronic locking and pass cards. With its rusted bolts and squeaking hinges, this was archaic by comparison.

From the notes of Dr Edwards: The prisoner is to stay in isolation whilst he is fully assessed.

Jimmy Eades: Taking me down a deserted corridor, the guards stopped by the door of a solitary cell. Outside the cell there's a puddle of what looks like blood and vomit, all lumpy and swirled together creating this beetroot coloured gloop.

The guards look at me, like there was no question, *just clean.* And with that they walked back to the heavy set door, leaving me to it.

I'm curious so I sidle up to the cell door and slowly go to peer through the small window, but a growl from inside the cell makes me jump and I return to my cleaning duties. That's Mooney alright, I keep thinking, praying the cell door is locked and hoping he hasn't seen me.

From the notes of Dr Edwards: He has been moved to the isolation cell near my office, however I have not been able to get close enough to conduct a full examination so I cannot ascertain if any of the blood on him is actually his own.

In due course he will calm. Until then I will observe through the cell door window.

Jimmy Eades: Dr Edwards and the Governor appear and start verbally tearing strips off each other. I keep my head down and clean the floor.

Peter Ball: The Governor thought he'd had it under control, nipped the trouble in the bud. Had he fuck. It was quiet, but that only meant you couldn't see the trouble. It was still there, brewing.

Jimmy Eades: The floor is cleaned and I'm knackered from all the scrubbing, so I bid my leave from the Doc and the Governor and take the stuff back to the cleaning cupboard in the basement. I wash out the bucket and mop, and I'm stacking them neatly away when I hear footsteps coming down the stairs.

We're on lockdown so I'm thinking it can only be a guard. You can imagine my shock when I heard Rich Webster's sneering voice over the hum of the generator.

Peter Ball: Even something as simple as a lockdown can be hard to strictly enforce. Not everyone plays by the same rules. It's a problem in all prisons.

Jimmy Eades: Rich and his brother, Mark, are talking to a third person. I'm hidden on the other side of the cleaning cupboard, tucked out of view.

"We want Mooney," Rich demands. "Our brother's on a life support and we want revenge."

"I can't get to him. He's in a medical isolation cell. He's in soliatry," a scared voice responds. "I have no access there. It was risky enough opening the doors and turning a blind eye when you got Forbes. I'm already under close watch. There's nothing I can do."

Peter Ball: It's almost a given that some of my colleagues are on the payroll of prisoners. Some get found out, some don't. It's not easy to flush them all out. And if you do, they'll only get replaced by another, either lured in by the money or coerced by some other means.

Jimmy Eades: My mop handle falls from the cupboard towards me. I reach out to catch it and stupidly knock over a bottle of floor cleaner. It clatters on the ground and within seconds Mark Webster has found me, giving me a look that is almost, but not quite, a smile.

I can remember his exact words, soft and eloquent, "Aren't you the proverbial bad penny?"

I couldn't have agreed with him more.

Rich Webster wades in and grabs me by the throat, pushing me against the wall.

"Well, well, you really are always in the wrong place at the wrong time." Rich squeezes harder and I gasp to find breath. His knee strikes my groin and I want to double over in pain, but he holds me straight. I try not to show fear in front of these two animals, but I fail miserably.

"We've got your card marked, Eades," he says, spitting his words in my face. "Can't be no coincidence you're always around. Are you fucking with us?"

I can't form words from my red raw throat so I shake my head. He smiles again, seeming to accept my denial.

"You run home now. Run back to your cell and this time remember that you saw us. Don't forget, as we'll see each other very soon." He loosened his grip on my throat before throwing me to the floor. I gasped loudly for air and looked up to the prison guard. His face was one of sympathy and frustration. He looked like he wanted to help, but for whatever reason was powerless to intervene. "When we need you, we'll come calling,"

Rich warned, kicking me in the side before walking away, leaving me on the floor holding my bruised ribs.

Peter Ball: Fear, intimidation, blackmail. The bastards will find a way to get to you.

Jimmy Eades: I'd never find peace in this place again.

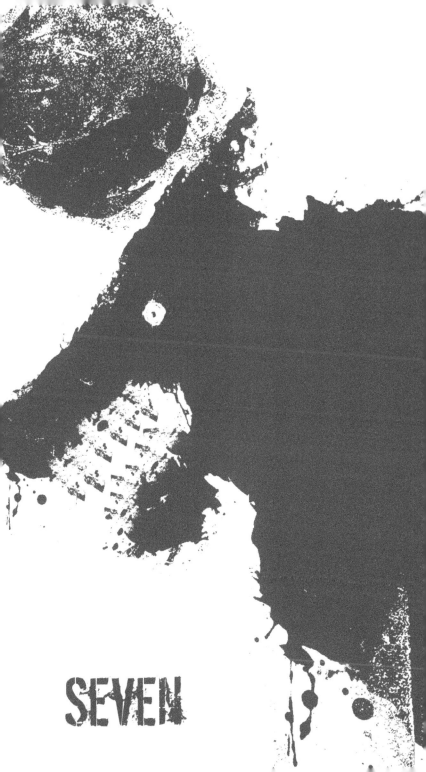

SEVEN

From the notes of Dr Edwards (Prison Doctor): I would like to report that the friction between myself and Governor Peel has eased over the weeks since I started my role here, but that would simply not be true. Whilst I understand the tragic circumstances with which the position I now hold initially became vacant, and whilst I have sympathy with the pain and shock they all must feel, I find this no excuse for the Governor's behaviour. His methods and views are outdated and I am certain he harbours resentment towards my gender. In short, Mr Peel is a dinosaur, one that sadly seems to have lived through the asteroid impact of modernity.

My advice has not been heeded until now, taking another violent incident in Darkdale for him to act on my instruction. I am hoping he sees results in my methods, and those results will lead to the building of trust.

The prisoner has already caused unrest in the prison population, and as predicted was swiftly moved to a solitary cell. I am grateful for the use of the cell next to the medical complex. This at least offers complete isolation within my control.

It seems the other prisoners have taken to calling him *Mad Dog*, a nickname he was given prior to this incarceration. He is uncooperative and unpleasant, with an ability to make me feel afraid. I have hidden this feeling, refusing to allow myself to succumb to it and yet, irrationally, I sense that he knows; like he can smell it. I believe I am not the only person to feel this way, yet no one is willing to talk about it. At least not to me.

Medically he is in a healthy condition, noted his body is pocked with scars, although the entry wounds of the tasers have healed over completely, despite his other scarring. He is a remarkable healer in this respect as the arterial puncture seems to have left no trace.

He's completely blind in his right eye, and the scar running across his face would suggest the nature of the original injury was from some kind of puncture wound. He is lucky the eyeball is still attached, although quite useless.

Amongst his disfigurements there is one of particular curiosity to me, a strange scarring on his bicep, one I cannot get close enough to examine.

It doesn't appear to be a tattoo, the wounds are too deep, too wild. Yet there seems to be some form of pattern, some idea of design that suggests it is not random.

Maybe I am just tired. Overthinking. Perhaps it's nothing more than a burn mark. However I am intrigued and would like a closer examination.

Transcript taken from the dictaphone of Dr Edwards (Prison Doctor):

(male voice): I wasn't always like this.

(female voice): How do you mean?

(m): Like this. I wasn't always this way. The monster behind my eyes.

(f): Monster?

(m): You've seen it. Felt it. If you haven't by now, you will.

(f): How?

(m): …I change. *It* changes me.

(f): Have you changed now?

(m): What do you think?

(f): That doesn't answer my question.

(m): I'm Mad Dog, I'm not your pet. You can't keep me here. They've failed before.

(f): Tell me about before.

(m): I won't play your games. I can smell your blood, even from this distance… and I want to drink it.

(f): Why would you want to do that?

(m): The cell door is no protection. The moon will be full again, and when it is, you'll see... You'll feel… and I'll feast.

From the notes of Dr Edwards: His words get under my skin. Even as I pack my bags to leave for the night, I can hear his casual threat echo in my thoughts.

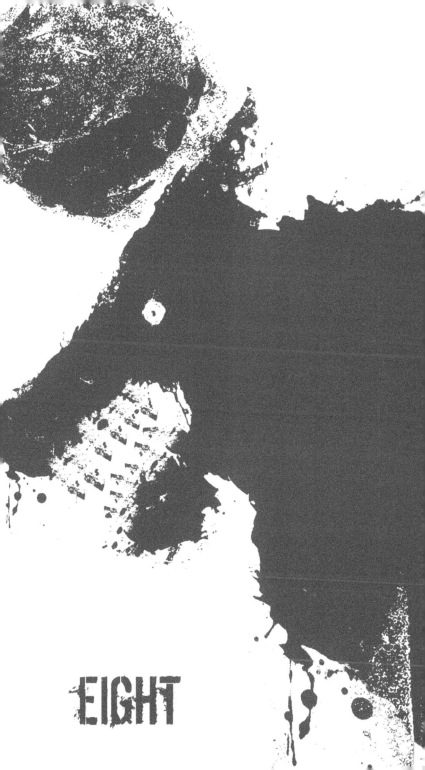

EIGHT

J. R. Park

From the notes of Dr Edwards (Prison Doctor): St Anne's hospital called this morning to inform us of the death of a prisoner.

Father Matthews (Prison Chaplain): It was symptomatic of the state of affairs inside the prison that we lost another life.

Peter Ball (Prison Guard): I don't mean to press on about it, but you have to understand, due to budget controls we had our hands tied. There was no money. No staff. The North Tower stood as a testament to the crumbling regime of Darkdale. Builders had started prepping but still weren't due to start properly for another few weeks. Until then the tower clung to the scaffolding. I swear you could hear it sway in the wind. We couldn't look after ourselves let alone the prisoners.

Jimmy Eades (Prisoner): I hadn't been allowed

visitors for weeks, I don't think anyone had. No one saw Mooney, but the stories still persisted. Did you know they found bite marks on that little girl he killed in the alley? They said his stool sample showed traces of human flesh. Man, that's so fucked up.

Jorge Wiles (Prisoner): Jimmy had eventually been given privilege rights back into the library. He was allowed to write again, which was good for him. I think Father Matthews had a little hand in that.

Jimmy Eades: I'd spent the last few weeks looking over my shoulder, wondering when the Websters would appear. I hadn't seen hide nor hair of them since they threatened me in the basement, and that made me even more nervous. I'd much rather keep my enemy in plain sight. But as the days wore on, that anxiousness started to fade.

Father Matthews: Jimmy was a troubled lad. I wanted to help where I could. Self-expression is better through writing than it is violence. I gave him a pen, one to keep safe and keep on him. No, I don't feel bad about it. My thinking was, should he lose his privileges again he'd always have some way to vent. To create.

Reform can only truly come through love.

Peter Ball: The Chaplain is blinded by his own compassion. Always has been. Even Darkdale failed to harden his soul.

Jimmy Eades: After a while things felt like they hit a

level of normality. I could still taste the hate in the air, it emanated from the walls, but it was part of the everyday. When something's a constant you begin to get used to it.

Jorge Wiles: We hadn't seen Mooney since the fight. I think that helped to calm things. We had no idea it was going to kick off again so badly.

Jimmy Eades: I was sat at a desk in the library, quietly scribbling away with the new pen Father Matthews had given me, when a letter was handed to me. I prayed I had guessed the sender correctly and tore the envelope open in a wave of rapture. *Hannah had written to me!* I poured over the letter, taking my time to read each sentence. Savour her every word. It brought everything back. Her face, her smell, her touch.

Jorge Wiles: He talked about Hannah a lot.

Jimmy Eades: So there I was, floating on a cloud. I guess I should have seen it coming.

Father Matthews: Happiness doesn't last long in hell. The demons make sure of that.

Jimmy Eades: I'm walking back to my cell to hide the letter away, when I'm grabbed from behind, a hand covering my mouth. I look across to the guard for help, but he pays no attention. Bastard must be paid off.

I knew whose hand it was before I even got a look at their face. Rich Webster, pulling me into the deserted shower room.

He holds me against the wall, his hand over my mouth keeping me quiet. His brother Mark eyes me.

"We told you we'd come when we needed you," Mark said pacing back and forth. "And today is that day. You have been chosen to aid us in the privilege of avenging our brother. Michael died in St Anne's hospital this morning. Mooney's got to be next."

He holds up a picture of Hannah. It's a recent photo, I can tell from the scarring on her face. They obviously had someone follow her. They threaten me, saying she's in danger if I didn't do what they said. I had no choice, I had to agree.

As I do, they both smile; then Mark explained his plan.

Tomorrow night whilst on my cleaning rounds I was to be handed a package. The package had to be treated carefully. It was a homemade explosive and potentially volatile. Keeping it in my trolley I'd wheel it down to the basement and pack my cleaning gear away, just like I usually do. In the basement, by the cleaning cupboard, is a door that leads to the emergency generator. This would be left unlocked. At six tomorrow night, before the night shift arrive and the tail end of the day shift are the only ones remaining, I was to place the explosive on the generator.

They tell me that since the incident in the North Tower, it's the only one working. The explosive isn't big enough to destroy it but should be enough to cripple it. Enough to compromise the electronic locks throughout the prison.

There's enough hatred in this place to send the inmates wild if they get a sniff of freedom. And in the melee, that's when they'll get their revenge. That's when they'll get Mooney.

Jorge Wiles: From that afternoon, Jimmy had this look in his eye, like he was hiding a secret. I wanted to press him on it, but was afraid he'd close down completely. I didn't want to lose him, not after he'd made such good progress.

Jimmy Eades: Before they let me go, Mark stopped pacing, looked me dead straight and said one more thing, another quote I recognised. "Be great in act, as you have been in thought." I smiled to show my recognition of the source. Rich elbowed me in the stomach, knocking the wind from my lungs. I think I threatened his intelligence, or maybe he just liked hurting people.

J. R. Park

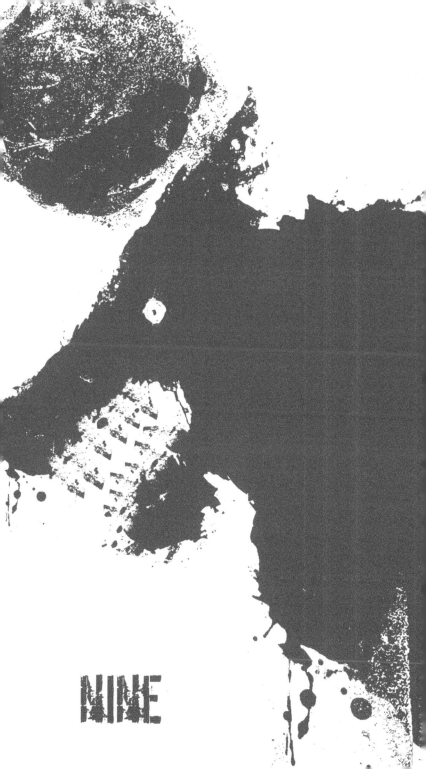

NINE

J. R. Park

From the notes of Dr Edwards (Prison Doctor): Forgive my messy handwriting, I've had to take a stronger dose than usual to calm me. Today has been quite the shock. I have seen things I never thought possible.

The prisoner emerged from his recently apathetic brooding and grew wildly animated today. A guard sent for me as the evening drew in, and I found him bouncing against the walls, screaming. He garbled that he was possessed, that tonight *we'd see*.

Curious about his delusion of possession, I pressed the matter with him, but he spoke no more, other than to demand the Chaplain.

Jimmy Eades (Prisoner): Darkdale was a centre of evil. Full of monsters. Monsters are real. Haven't you got that yet?

From the notes of Dr Edwards: The Chaplain sat with

him; calming his mood.

I observed through the view hole as the two spoke. Mooney repeated the story I'd previously recorded. He described a coming of another nature, a beast inside him that would take his body and mind when the full moon shone. "Could you help, Father?" he asked, showing a frailty I had not witnessed from him before. "Can you rid the demon inside of me?"

The Chaplain read passages from the bible as the prisoner lay down and listened intently. Eventually his words soothed the agitated inmate, and I watched his breathing grow steady as slowly he drifted off to sleep.

Father Matthews (Prison Chaplain): "For God gave us a spirit not of fear but of power and love and self-control." 2 Timothy 1:7

From the notes of Dr Edwards: Father Matthews quietly left, but I held my vigil, determined to find out what would happen as the night drew in and the moon illuminated his cell.

I did not have to wait long before the prisoner woke with a start. He looked towards the window and cried with a terrified anguish. Like a victim of rabies, his mouth began to froth; a foamy drool pouring down his chin that he jutted forward as if trying to rid himself of some foul taste.

Jimmy Eades: I don't know how it starts. But you can imagine it, can't you?

From the notes of Dr Edwards: I tore myself away

from what I saw and ran towards my office. Terrified out of my mind, I panicked, petrified his door wouldn't hold. I had to get help. I had to get a guard.

Father Matthews: I've seen all types of confused and lost souls in my time. And I've also seen things you can't explain. Felt things that just aren't right. Possession is very real.

Jimmy Eades: You can imagine Mooney, dropping to his knees and hair thickening on his back. His shoulders growing broader, forcing his chest to expand, amid the sound of snapping as his skeleton reconfigures to something more animal in shape.

His arms growing longer and his hands bigger. His fingernails thicken and extend out from his skin. Their tips reforming into points, like monstrous claws.

From the notes of Dr Edwards: I searched through my drawers and found my panic button. I have such a bad habit of leaving it around the place. My own fault for feeling too comfortable.

I went to press it, but something stopped me. A thought: as terrified as I was, if I called a guard what would happen?

They'd beat him. He'd shut down. I'd lose contact. This would help neither him nor me. I needed to know more.

Jimmy Eades: His cheeks develop cracks across the skin. Bleeding profusely, they turn into awful gashes that split wider until suddenly his jaw shoots forward, protruding from his face like a dog's muzzle. His teeth continue to grow until they look like daggers and his eyes change colour; his pupils contracting to a cat-like slit.

From the notes of Dr Edwards: Composing myself, and putting trust in the security of his cell, I left my office and slowly made my way along the corridor; unnerved by the silence that greeted me.

Father Matthews: You don't need my expert opinion of the esoteric to know there was something very, very wrong with him.

Jimmy Eades: You will believe.

From the notes of Dr Edwards: As I approached his cell I could see the outlined silhouette of his back in the corner of the room. I stood still and watched. My jaw clenched as I felt an unbearable tension. Slowly he turned to face me and I felt beads of sweat roll down my temple.

I went to speak, but instead a gasp left my mouth.

He leapt at the door; his teeth like those of a dog's, bared at the sealed exit that he hammered against for his freedom. He snarled at me through the cell door window, a wild storm of fury, and yet I couldn't work out if it was an expression of anger or pain. I stumbled backwards, unsure of his strength and concerned once more that the cell would not protect me from this creature.

His facial scar was still clear despite the hair that

covered his face. His blind eye shone green in contrast to the watery silver of his left. The light giving them the appearance of reflecting qualities; like that of an animal's.

He howled and attacked the door again, tearing at the panels and clawing at the walls. His focus was fixed, looking at me like I was nothing more than a piece of meat; his exposed canines and drooling mouth leaving no question as to his intentions should he escape his confinement.

Jimmy Eades: Monsters are real, and prisons are the first place you'll find them.

From the notes of Dr Edwards: Thankfully the door held him, and the solitary confinement did enough to mute the cries of the damned.

I tried to talk to him, but he showed no signs of understanding anything I said. Eventually my voice went hoarse and I couldn't watch him any longer as fear once again got the better of me. I turned and slumped against the wall, not wanting to leave this fascinating subject but too frightened to keep him in my gaze.

I waited until the noises tailed off, and as dawn grew I awoke, finding I had slept outside the cell. Inside, the prisoner was naked and sleeping peacefully.

This time I did call the guards – but didn't explain the sight I had seen. Had I seen it?

Was it just a dream? A hallucination? A contagious, psychotic hysteria brought on by the ramblings of the prisoner?

With enquiries into the violence he's caused I'm

frightened we'll lose this man; that he'll be taken to another facility. I don't want that to happen, so last night's events go unrecorded save for my own personal notes.

I have to understand what happened.

Tonight I shall be prepared.

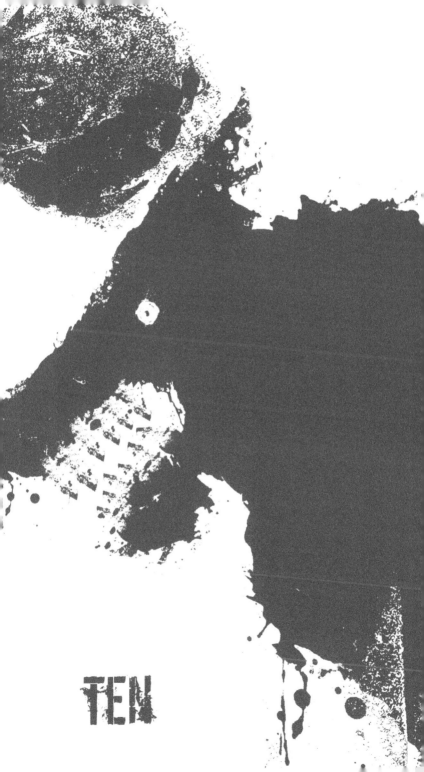

TEN

From the notes of Dr Edwards (Prison Doctor): He awoke with seemingly little memory of the night before, or at least no memories he was willing to talk about. That being said he made no comments about the huge marks that had been ripped into the door. I believe he knows more than he's letting on.

Jorge Wiles (Prisoner): Jimmy seemed more agitated than normal when I saw him that morning. I didn't want to pry, that's not my style. But I knew something was up.

Jimmy Eades (Prisoner): I woke up with a feeling of dread in the pit of my stomach.

From the notes of Dr Edwards: I explained to the prisoner that I would restrain him in a chair this evening, with straps to his wrists, ankles, waist and head. He was not resistant to this, in fact he seemed almost grateful.

Throughout the day he began to open up a little, describing last night like flashes of a distant memory, as if trying to recall a drunken night out.

Peter Ball (Prison Guard): It was just a normal day. Perhaps too normal. Looking back my spider-sense should have been tingling.

Jimmy Eades: I couldn't eat. I was too nervous. My mind went over the instructions again and again. I visibly shook with adrenalin as the afternoon turned to evening and I set about with my trolley and mop.

Transcript taken from the dictaphone of Dr Edwards: The prisoner has resisted any offers of food. He claims he is not hungry. I surmise the beast inside is waiting to be fed. God that sounds so stupid. Tonight we'll see how foolish I'm being.

Jimmy Eades: As my duties come to an end I watch a pair of hands slip a brown parcel into the empty bucket on my trolley. I don't even look up to see who makes the drop off. I do not care. Swallowing back my fear, I fill the bucket with spare cloths, hiding the package. I don't need to look. I already know what's in it.

Transcript taken from the dictaphone of Dr Edwards: It is a cloudy night, and I hope this doesn't disrupt the lunar effects on the prisoner. Maybe the subject can be motivated through suggestion. He looks pensive. Perhaps my mood is reflecting back onto him.

Jimmy Eades: I take the trolley down to the basement. It's empty. There is never anyone around, but tonight I keep checking over my shoulder.

I lift up the pile of cloths and open the parcel. The device is crude and much smaller than I imagined. A wire protrudes from a digital Casio watch face and into something wrapped in plastic. I step towards the door, half expecting it to be locked. It swings open easily; the noise of the generator grows louder.

Transcript taken from the dictaphone of Dr Edwards: The prisoner is beginning to convulse in the chair like he is having a fit. His face suggests he is in pain and he's grunting as he spasms. His cheeks are bulging, his forehead pulsating. His muscles are swelling, straining at the straps. His teeth! My god, his teeth!

Jimmy Eades: No one told me where to place the bomb so I walk around the generator trying to select the best spot. I was never gifted with much technical know-how, so I make a guess and fix it on the side, near a vent and control panel. I'm hoping the more components it's near the more damage it's going to cause. I press the button on the watch face and hightail it out of the room. According to the readout I've got two minutes to get clear. My heart is pounding against my chest like a sledgehammer.

Transcript taken from the dictaphone of Dr Edwards: He's pulling at his straps. He seems even more aggressive than yesterday. I guess he's even hungrier tha- Shit! He's just broken through the straps like they were paper. Oh fuck, fuck, fuck! He's ripped them clean from the chair. The subject is on his feet. He's- fuck!

Fuck, that was close! He's just slammed against the door. It rattled on its hinges, but it held. Breathe Nic, come on, breathe. It held last night, it'll hold again.

Jimmy Eades: Two minutes might seem like a long time, but not to my jelly-like legs. The adrenaline has taken my sense of balance, disorientating me as I try to run clear. My limbs feel like air. I'm scared to trust them.

I'm only just at the top of the stairs as the explosion rips through the generator room. The lights around the prison flicker on and off, struggling to stay illuminated. The generator continues to limp on, but quickly begins to overheat. The electricity supply falters, then the lights go down. A click echoes around the complex signifying the guard's worst nightmare.

The doors have unlocked.

All of them.

For a moment a stunned silence hangs over the prison.

It's broken by the sound of a bestial howl. The noise echoes in the open spaces of Darkdale. I look up to see Mark Webster open his cell door and scream at the top of his lungs.

"Brothers, we are free! Seize our moment whilst we are in fortune's favour!"

The demons had done it.

And I had helped them.

We'd opened the gates of hell.

ELEVEN

Jorge Wiles (Prisoner): The air felt thinner as the doors unbolted. My breathing shallowed and my heart started going ten to the dozen. I felt giddy, and although I tried to stay in my cell, to keep out of the way, I remember being pulled outside; being compelled to see what was happening by a force that was stronger than me.

From the notes of Dr Edwards (Prison Doctor): Human beings are a social species, evolved to live in groups. But we are also a competitive creature and destruction is as natural to us as unity. Never is this seen so clear as in a prison population. Within the same environment, wearing the same clothes and living the same routine, groups are still formed. Leaders are created. Hostilities made.

Small groups can be controlled, but the dangers lie in a gathering, a crowd; strength in numbers. Unfortunately strength and size rarely equates to clear thinking. Usually fuelled from an underlying emotion, whose coming to the fore has been brought about by one singular event, this emotive response can be contagious and dangerously heightened.

Peter Ball (Prison Guard): They were fucking animals.

Jimmy Eades (Prisoner): I'd never seen anything like it. They rushed from their cells, antagonised by the cries of Mark Webster stirring them up into a fit of anger. The guards were easily overwhelmed and were set upon by the rushing mob who beat them back with their bare hands. Those guards that were able to get a first crack with their batons only managed to excite the baying crowd further causing an even wilder hostility.

Jorge Wiles: I watched from the second floor walkway as blood was splattered across the walls, teeth were smashed into brickwork and heads were kicked in until they cracked.

Peter Ball: Seeing the state of those bodies…
God rest their souls, the poor bastards. If I'd have been on shift, no doubt I wouldn't be here talking to you now.

Jimmy Eades: Fingers were bitten off as keys and torches were brutally pulled from the guards. The crowd scrambled for the exit, attacking any resistance that was left with a wave of fists and bodies. All I could do was watch in awe, terrified to move from the spot.

Jorge Wiles: "Get the nonces!" someone shouted from the level below me.

From the notes of Dr Edwards: A rioting crowd is as unpredictable as it is spontaneous. It has no history, no sentiment, no consequence. It only exists for a brief moment in time, and therefore is unbound by the normal social constructs that surround it.

As witnessed in many documented riots, the anonymity of a crowd makes it easier for people to perform atrocious acts of brutality. Within normal society this is of concern, but within a prison population where brutality is a way of life, this is positively alarming.

Jorge Wiles: Soon after, I saw bloodied faces looking up at me, being choked on the railings below. I remember wincing as I caught sight of some poor wretch's nose-less face. A broken body, all limbs at wrong angles, sailed through the air and landed on the mesh below the walkway. He twitched, but I couldn't tell if that was nerve impulses or a conscious reaction to pain. Alive or dead, he was sprawled out on the chain links, dripping blood onto the floor below. A chair was ripped from the floor and thrown towards him; one of its legs punctured his cheek and tore through his face. I'd seen some fucked up shit in my time, and I knew this was only the beginning.

A barrage of bed posts, fire extinguishers, whatever they could wrestle from the fittings, where hurled towards the poor bastard. I turned and headed down the stairs, unable to watch as I heard the crack of his skull and the slop of brain matter hitting the floor.

Jimmy Eades: It was all going on around me. I didn't know what to do. My only thought was to escape, to flee this madness. So I ran, following the crowd as they streamed towards the prison gates.

Jorge Wiles: I don't know why, but I was worried about Jimmy. He'd be an easy target, so I headed to the ground floor, desperately looking for the lad.

Jimmy Eades: The corridor leading to the visitor area was already unlocked by the time I reached it. A mangled body of a guard lay slumped through the bars. His arms had been snapped just below the elbows and weaved around the metal poles. His head visibly forced through. The man's skull was a misshapen lump; fragmented and beaten until it had been squashed into the opening between the bars. His cracked jaw was snapped in three places and hung uselessly beside his neck.

I gasped as he slowly moved, trying to reach out for help, but made no attempt to stop.

As I ran outside, I felt the rain and the cold October air. The fresh taste of freedom was beautiful, but short lived.

Peter Ball: Governor Peel wasn't a stupid man. With a weakened infrastructure and still feeling the effects of the first incident, he'd set up an emergency response unit, just in case something like this was to happen.

Jimmy Eades: Suddenly we were all blinded as these

huge spotlights shone on us. There was some kind of buzz; a command shouted over a loud speaker, but through the wind and noise I didn't have a clue what they were saying.

Peter Ball: The taskforce was mobile in a matter of minutes of the alarms being raised. Good thing too, otherwise they'd have all broken free.

Jimmy Eades: Shots fired out and I watched a prisoner drop in front of me. Blood was pissing from his shoulder as he writhed on the ground in pain. He caught hold of my leg, but I kicked him off. I'm not normally like that. I'm a nice guy. But as I heard another bullet whistle past my ear and drop another man behind me, I only cared for myself.

Peter Ball: We were up and active even before the press could get on the scene. Good thing too. Meant we could dispense some real crowd control before those do-gooding humanitarians caught wind of it.

Rubber bullets rarely cause fatalities, anyway. But they'll leave one hell of a bruise.

Jimmy Eades: With nowhere else to go I instinctively ran back towards Darkdale, away from the bullets.

I was fighting through the crowd, but as the understanding of what was happening rippled through the ranks, it wasn't long before they'd all turned tail and starting heading the same way.

With each shot came the scream of another prisoner dropping to the ground. By the time we got back to the entrance I reckon there were at least twenty dead. Maybe more.

Peter Ball: Boo fucking hoo. I hear a lot of crap about the way that was handled. Don't trust Jimmy, he's a fucking liar. We used rubber bullets, not live ones. Fatalities were few. It was all documented in the inquiry that followed, but fuck me, we had to use something. Those guys had brutally killed a few dozen guards. You want those monsters loose on the streets? This is Darkdale you know, not some halfway house for tax evaders. The guys in there are mean. Real fucking mean.

Yeah it was aggressive, but it wasn't deadly. I'm standing by the Governor on that one. He saved a lot of lives that day, believe me.

Jorge Wiles: Panic reaches a whole new height as I get to the entrance and see a crush of people pushing back in, whilst those inside are pulling up chairs and tables to form a barricade.

I'm looking all over the place for Jimmy, but there's too many of us. A sea of faces, bleeding and shouting and trying to find safety.

Eventually the door is sealed shut. The sound of those still trapped outside hammer on the great steel door as the barricade is piled against it. Poor bastards, I thought, hoping if Jimmy didn't get back in he'd get picked up by the cops once they'd finished their trigger happy meet and greet.

Jimmy Eades: The crowd is slowing me down and my heart begins to sink as I watch the door closing. With a last ditch effort, I push past all those around me, kicking and biting to keep them at bay until I get to my goal. A bullet pings off the entrance and my hand stings from the reverberation of its impact, but I'm determined not to give up.

I feel someone grab at my thigh and pull me backwards. Without looking behind me, I kick out and feel the heavy impact of my foot on his face. Something crunches against the sole of my shoe, but if he screamed it was lost in the wash of agony that buzzed about me.

His grip on me instantly loosened and I pull myself into the prison, quickly climbing to my feet and falling in line with the crowd.

Looking up I see Mark Webster standing on an overturned drinks machine, watching with a satisfied smile as those around him tear furniture and fittings from their place and toss them together into a makeshift barricade. I try my hardest to disappear into the melee but he spies me and jumps down to where I'm stood.

"It's glorious, isn't it?" he says as his smile widens. "Can you hear? Some of them have taken to the roof! Classic, don't you think? I will join them for the view whilst you do what you need to."

Confused at his last sentence, it all became clear when a hand viscously gripped my shoulder and spun me around.

"Alright you fucker." It was Rich Webster with a posse behind him. "Come with me. You know which cell Mad Dog's in. Come show me and the boys."

And with that I was forced to march back into the holding cells of Darkdale; to lead these fools into the very depths of hell and meet the devil himself.

TWELVE

Peter Ball (Prison Guard): The Governor was understandably pissed.

Constable Richard Hoskins (Firearms Officer): I'd never met Darkdale's Governor Peel until that night. I'd heard of him; he had quite the reputation. As soon as he started barking orders I knew he wouldn't get on very well with my boss. I was right.

Inspector Geoffrey Thompson (Firearms Officer): I have no comment to make on the matter.

Constable Richard Hoskins: Under instruction of the Governor we'd opened fire on the hostiles. We'd originally planned to fire warning shots, but with a rampaging horde of murderers running towards you it's hard to keep your nerve. Trigger fingers get a little twitchy.

Anyhow, our attack had the desired effect and sent

them running. When Inspector Thompson arrived, he blew up.

"You got here, then?" the Governor greeted him with a cheeky put down. I tried not to smile, but couldn't help but smirk. My eyes were trained on the entrance to Darkdale, so thankfully my weapon hid most of my face.

Peter Ball: I stepped aside. Best to keep out of the way when the big boys lock horns.

Constable Richard Hoskins: "I came as quick as I could," the Inspector said. He was still catching his breath. You could tell he'd ran from his car. Not the fittest man on the force. "What's going on?" he asked.

"We've got ourselves a full scale riot," the Governor said in a dismissive, *isn't it obvious*, kind of tone.

"You must be getting used to this sort of thing," came the retort.

The Inspector gave as good as he got.

Peter Ball: I paced between the ranks, letting them argue it out between themselves for a moment. I couldn't make out what they were saying from where I was, but the wild arm waving was clear: the Inspector was not happy about the liberal use of gunfire, even if they were rubber bullets.

Just what we needed. A bleeding-heart leftie in our own ranks.

Constable Richard Hoskins: The pair were arguing right next to me. Inspector Thompson screaming about the correct use of force, whilst the Governor explaining that we'd only used it to halt the rush; that a lot had been captured and were already detained; that some of his men were still inside.

It was about then the roof tiles started landing at our feet.

Peter Ball: The bastards had climbed up onto the roof and started hurling slates at us. I approached Governor Peel to understand the next course of action. The North Tower was already dangerous, and with prisoners climbing on top of it, there was no way we could use it as an entry point. Especially when they started tugging at the scaffolding.

Constable Richard Hoskins: We pulled back a little to keep out of range of the projectiles. The spotlights were aimed at the rooftop, and that's when we saw it.

Sergeant Kate Shaw (Firearms Officer): There were calls on the radio for a chopper, but the request was denied. The wind was howling and the rain was coming down sideways.

Inspector Geoffrey Thompson: I repeat, I have no comment.

Peter Ball: The spotlights shine on the roof, and to begin with we're all having trouble making out what we're looking at. The figures are all glowing a bright white against the light as they scurry about, trying to avoid the glare. Then we catch sight of two men stood defiantly on the edge of the North Tower. They're waving to us; beating their chests and sticking their fingers up.

They've got something by their feet. It's large. Heavy.

Sergeant Kate Shaw: My team are stood further back, so from our angle we actually get a better view. As they lift up the object we can see the length of the scaffolding pole.

And a pair of legs kicking wildly underneath it.

Constable Richard Hoskins: The bickering between the two superiors stop when they become as hypnotised as the rest of us at the image of these two prisoners lifting another man above their heads.

Sergeant Kate Shaw: The rain is beating even harder, but there's still enough visibility to make out the prison guard uniform. The white shirt, stained pink with blood, and his black tie, flapping in the wind.

Peter Ball: I must have been the last to understand what was going on, because I couldn't make out what it was until they'd thrown him over the edge.

Sergeant Kate Shaw: He falls for a moment and then suddenly stops, dangling in mid-air; suspended by a cable.

Peter Ball: He's just hanging there, his arms outstretched and tied to a scaffolding pole like he's been crucified.

Constable Richard Hoskins: I'm one of the few close enough to see the full horror of what's happened. The scaffolding pole's been driven through his shoulders. In through one, under his chest and out the other side. I can't imagine the agony. They must have punctured a lung, maybe cracked some ribs, split an artery. There was blood pissing out from his body in these huge arcs and pouring from his mouth.

The cable pulls tight stopping the guard's fall. He swings wildly in the wind and then there's this awful crack as his collar bone snaps.

Peter Ball: The wind fractures the sound, but you can hear the poor guy whimpering.

Constable Richard Hoskins: The cable and the scaffolding, they're both slowly ripping through the guard. Centimetre by centimetre. Without any bone to keep the pole in place, we watch as his muscle and skin relinquish under the strain, slowly tearing a huge hole just below his neck.

There's guys below running around, screaming and shouting, trying to think of some way to help the poor fucker. But there's nothing we can do.

As the last strands of skin finally give out, there's a gargled scream and the guard drops to his death.

Sergeant Kate Shaw: You don't want to know the detail. That's just sick. Dental records couldn't identify the mess that was left behind.

Peter Ball: The bastards above are shouting; jeering at us, like this is all some sort of game. We're all in shock for a moment, but it doesn't take long to turn into anger.

Sergeant Kate Shaw: The airwaves start blowing up with a tirade of angry commands. "Get me a fucking chopper", "Close the streets", "Find a way in now!"

Within the melee we get an instruction from Inspector Thompson. They need a team to infiltrate Darkdale. I knew we'd get the command. Me and my team. We're the best. It's what we do.

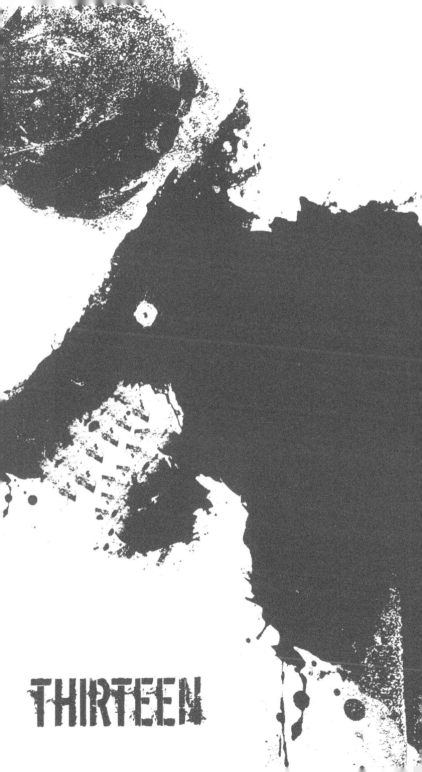

THIRTEEN

J. R. Park

Transcript taken from the dictaphone of Dr Edwards (Prison Doctor): I am having to speak very quietly. I hope the microphone is still able to pick up my voice.

Jimmy Eades (Prisoner): I was amazed how the din of the riot subsided as we walked into the corridor reserved for solitary confinement.

Jorge Wiles (Prisoner): Solitary confinement was probably the oldest part of Darkdale. That, coupled with the budget constraints meaning it wasn't upgraded with the rest of prison, made it feel really old. Kind of archaic. I hated going down there. It was always cold. Always gave me the creeps.

Father Matthews (Prison Chaplain): The Governor had to make a call. "Why waste money on it? Solitary conferment is supposed to be a punishment", was his attitude.

Transcript taken from the dictaphone of Dr Edwards: If I don't survive, it's important this recording be preserved; that my work is documented.

Jimmy Eades: It took Webster's men a while to find the right key, but it was the only way in. This place didn't run on electronic locking like the rest.

Father Matthews: There were only a few cells down there. It was the old part of the prison, running just off from the medical wing and the guard's mess. Having the finery of the mess so close to the squalid conditions of Solitary was something I could imagine the Governor relishing in. A twisted, psychological punishment.

It was very *him*.

Transcript taken from the dictaphone of Dr Edwards: All that I have noted on this tape has been observed with the utmost sincerity.

Jimmy Eades: "It's at the end of the corridor," I tell them. "The last cell on the left."

I stand by the entrance of the corridor and shine the torch I stole from a bleeding guard's corpse into the mess room. There's a dictaphone lying in the middle of the floor but I think nothing of it. I just wanted to get in and out as quickly as I could. Beside it lies a panic button the guards carry. *A bit useless now*, I muse and smirk.

When Rich Webster ordered me to follow them to

the cell, my heart sank.

Transcript taken from the dictaphone of Dr Edwards: I hope it is of some use in understanding the peculiarities of the patient.

Jimmy Eades: The noises of the riot are almost completely lost in the stifling silence of the dark, dingy corridor. The other cells appear empty. My thoughts are racing. *Did the doctor move them all? Or are they too scared to make a sound?*

The only thing to break the near serenity are our cautious footsteps. We're all scared out of our minds, but no one wants to admit it. Even Rich Webster seems a little slow in his stride, but he continues to keep his chest puffed out and his head held high. The guy was a complete psychopath.

"Mooney," he half sings as he scans his torch beam around the passageway. "I'm looking for you."

By the time we reach the end of the corridor, our feet are splashing in puddles. It's so dark that we don't notice the colour of the liquid coating the floor. Our eyes and torches are all trained on the cell door in front of us. There's a hole ripped through it. *Right through it!* Right through the bottom of the door.

Who could do that?

Peter Ball (Prison Guard): I don't care what anyone else says. There was no way he tore through a cell door. You've seen the thickness of them, right?

Father Matthews: A lot of people have said a lot of

things. Facts get confused, stories get embellished. But the place was old. It was in bad need of repair. What happened with the generators already told us that.

If any cell doors had taken a beating over the years, it would have been those in Solitary.

Jimmy Eades: We all know it's a futile gesture, but we carry on to the entrance of the bust-open cell. I mean, we all knew it was going to be empty. But we had to see it for ourselves. We had to be sure.

Transcript taken from the dictaphone of Dr Edwards: As to what has just happened, I don't know for sure. The power went down and the prisoners began to riot.

Jimmy Eades: But it wasn't empty.

Transcript taken from the dictaphone of Dr Edwards: I'm hiding behind a desk in the guard's mess. Somehow the subject has escaped. The sound of cries and gunfire are echoing down the corridor, but the thing I can hear most is the beast. It growls as it stalks me. I swear it's tracking my scent.

Jimmy Eades: The cell was splattered from floor to ceiling with blood. Literally splattered. Chunks of meat, chewed and gnarled, still clinging to pieces of splintered bone and dribbling down the walls like they'd been thrown from an explosion.

I see a face. Sorry, I see part of a face. An eye and half a nose still held together by a sliver of cheekbone.

There's something familiar about the green eye looking up at me through a veil of ravaged meat, but it doesn't click until I look away.

One of Rich's gang doubles over beside me and spews all down his legs.

I feel myself reacting in the same way so turn my gaze from the horror in the cell. It's then I notice a shredded lab coat at the edge of the corridor. My torch scans further. I see a shoe bitten in half, a clump of hair pulled from its roots, a rag of clothing torn in two. There'd been a struggle, but the aggressor had clearly won.

The clothes were a giveaway, but when I saw a pair of severed digits down by my feet, I was left in no doubt. There was only one person in this place I knew that wore such a flashy wedding ring.

Transcript taken from the dictaphone of Dr Edwards: Good God. If I don't make it out of here, tell Derrick I love him.

Jimmy Eades: Then we heard the growl.

J. R. Park

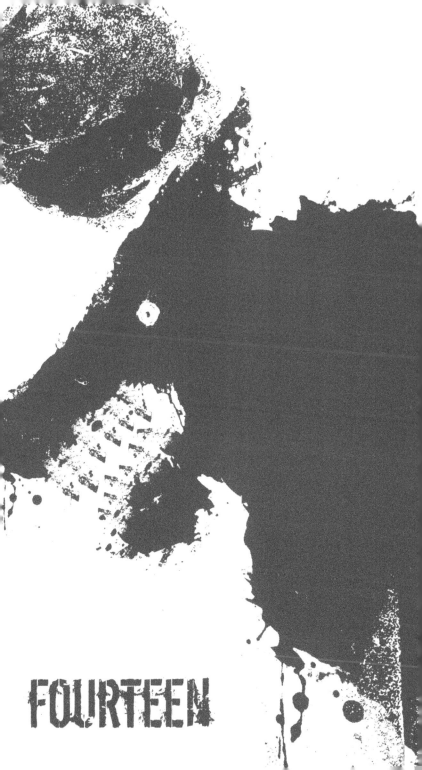

FOURTEEN

Sergeant Kate Shaw (Firearms Officer): The ground floor was heavily fortified. Barricades had been piled up against all the windows and doors. We needed to get higher, to find an access point, and time was running out. The longer we sat around devising plans and strategies, the more chance they had to prepare; to hole themselves in for good.

We needed to be swift. Our only chance was to take them early on, whilst they were still figuring out what to do.

Constable Richard Hoskins (Firearms Officer): The North Tower was swaying in the wind. The more scaffolding the prisoners prised off, the more unstable it became.

Sergeant Kate Shaw: The tower was a no go, but a fire escape ran up the east side of the main building. It was risky, but if we moved quickly we could ascend the stairs and make our way in through the upper levels.

Peter Ball (Prison Guard): They were brave, I'll give them that. The windows were dark on the east side with little signs of activity. The spotlights were kept away from that area in a bid not to attract attention.

Sergeant Kate Shaw: We kept to the shadows, sticking tight to the walls as we followed the perimeter of the prison. I don't know when we were first spotted. It might have been from someone on the roof, or maybe some eagle-eared inmate heard our light pitter-patter over the steel staircase.

Eagle-eared, is that even a saying?

Anyway, I still haven't got to the bottom of what exactly happened, but we were almost two stories up when we knew we'd been rumbled.

Jorge Wiles (Prisoner): I remember hearing this huge cheer and a crowd rushing by me. I stopped one of them to ask what was happening.

"The pigs are trying to sneak in," he told me. "They've been caught on the fire escape. Come on."

Sergeant Kate Shaw: Roof tiles hurtled down onto the team, smashing against our riot armour. The first one cracked against my helmet and brought me to the floor, knocking the wind out of me for a moment. I recovered quickly and climbed back to my feet. This was not a place for weakness.

We did our best to avoid the rest of the missiles, but we were cornered halfway between floors. The stairs blocked any clean shot we could get without fear of ricochet, and all doors and windows were either just below us, or just above us. Whether it was luck or judgement, the bastards had us at our most vulnerable.

Peter Ball: Darkdale prison was already falling to pieces before the rioters got their hate-fuelled hands on it. I'm surprised that fire escape stayed up as long as it did.

Sergeant Kate Shaw: The steel walkway started to sway. Through brute force and sheer numbers the prisoners shook the structure; pushing and pulling until they loosened it from the wall. As the ground beneath us bowed and wobbled, we had trouble keeping our balance. I fired a few blind shots into a window of the second floor, breaking the glass, and made a run for it, ordering my team to follow suit.

With my head down, I half ran, half stumbled as I forced my way through the barrage of projectiles and over the warping structure that was collapsing around me.

Leaping as I got to the edge, my fingertips caught the window frame and I held my breath as I felt fresh air beneath my feet. The platform had completely given way.

Pulled clear of the wall and unable to keep its own shape, it crashed to the ground.

Constable Richard Hoskins: By the time we got round to the east side the fire escape was nothing but a pile of scrap in the dirt. I didn't even stop to look at the broken limbs that protruded out from the twisted metal. My gun sights were trained on the prisoners up top, my mission to drive them back from the edge and halt their barrage on the wounded below.

Peter Ball: The kid gloves had come off. There were no rubber bullets now.

Sergeant Kate Shaw: My feet scrabbled for grip against the wet surface of the prison wall. I panicked as I failed to find any purchase and felt my fingers slip from the window ledge.

A hand caught me and pulled me up. It was PC Harrington. One of my team.

He pulled me into the safety of the building and we took a moment to catch our breath. I clocked three had made it with me. Constables Harrington, Hawkins and Mew.

Darkdale roared with the cries of angry prisoners; their voices booming down the empty corridors.

We had to move quickly. It wouldn't be long before a recon party came down here to check for any survivors. After all, we hadn't exactly made the most discrete of entrances.

Hawkins reached for his radio, but I stopped him. We needed to sink into the shadows. Let stealth be our weapon once more.

Peering over the edge, it was clear that our point of exit would not be the same as our point of entry. We had only one choice: to head further into the prison.

With a depleted team it wasn't going to be easy, but I was with the best. We had the tools and we had the talent.

We also had no choice.

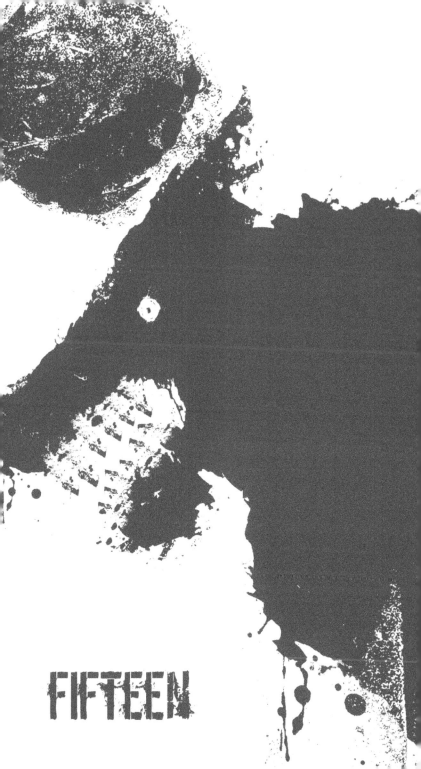

FIFTEEN

Jimmy Eades (Prisoner): The guys are flashing their torches all over the place meaning we aren't really focusing on anything. A glimpse of a blood-red puddle, a shredded piece of clothing, a rusting pipe; we weren't seeing anything clearly. It was like the world's worst zoetrope.

Another growl. Louder this time, sending them all into an even wilder panic. Except for Rich Webster. The crazy bastard held his ground and his nerve.

"Come on you fucker," he called out into the darkness. "I ain't scared of you."

My beam found a bloody footprint on the wall. Then a hand print, then another footprint. I tracked them, finding another, then another. The prints ran up the wall and across the ceiling.

That's when we saw him.

His eyes shone as my torchlight caught him, curled into the corner and staring down at us; his bare feet digging into the wall, keeping him suspended so high up.

His clothes had been torn off and his muscles rippled through a covering of hair. A *thick* covering of hair. All over.

He looked so different.

He'd changed, just like I told you. Just like I said it had happened.

Don't give me that smile; that condescending nod, like you know more than me. You think I'm bonkers, but I'm not. What I'm telling you is real.

Wipe that grin off your face and keep an open mind. If not, that's all you're getting from me.

One smirk and we're done.

Don't say I didn't warn you.

We good…?

Trust me. You will believe.

Okay. Well for starters his mouth looked all wrong: too big and rammed full of these huge fangs. His hands were over-sized too, and as one reached out towards us I caught sight of his claw-like fingers. They dripped with blood. Fresh blood.

His ears grew out, taller than his head and he snarled, curling back his lips and exposing his teeth like a rabid dog. Like a wolf.

I know. Sounds stupid, right?

But I swear, that's what I saw.

He studied us for a moment, his glowing eyes brighter than our own torches; and we all stood still, dumb-founded as we tried to make sense at what we were looking at. His muscles bulged as they strained to keep him suspended, making him look even bigger, even more terrifying.

A low growl increased in volume and ferocity, and I

remember mouthing the words, "What the fuck?" before he launched his attack.

With an ear splitting roar, he leapt at us. I threw my torch to the ground, put my head down and ran straight towards the exit. Yeah, it was towards the monster, but what choice did I have? It was either that or wait like a sitting duck and get ripped to pieces. That's what happened to the others. I didn't see it after he leapt over me, but I heard their screams; heard the sound of shredding clothes as his claws sliced through skin like soft butter. I heard the wet slap of bodies hitting the floor as he ripped into flesh and tore open throats, releasing sprays of arterial blood in fountains of crimson. I heard the crack of breaking bones, the agonising wails as arms were snapped and skulls shattered.

They didn't stand a chance.

All the while Rich Webster is screaming at him, "Come on you bastard. You hairy cunt. I'll fucking fix you!"

I think that psycho went down still shouting obscenities, but there was no way I was waiting it out to see who the winner of that slugfest was. My money was on the hairy monster in the corner, know what I mean?

I reached the door and slammed it shut behind me, faintly hearing Rich's final fear-drenched scream as the door went click. I turned the handle, but didn't have the key to lock it. Stupidly I paused for a moment and leant against the metal door, fleetingly thinking I'd found some respite. The next thing I know the door's buckling behind me; shaking on its hinges. Bang, bang, bang, it's going. Mad Dog pulverising the other side; trying his hardest to bust through.

Blood pours in rivers from underneath the door, slopping through the gaps and soaking my shoes, making it hard to find grip as I fight against the onslaught on the other side.

And then it all stops for a moment. I dare not breathe as I try to figure out what's happening. I listen intently for a sign of movement, jumping with fright as I hear the creature roar. I'm gone, already running before he starts on the door again and finds a way out.

It seemed crazy that I was running back into the heart of the prison, searching for a large group; that I'd seek solace in a crowd of murderers. But that was the only option I had left. Despite the atrocities they had committed at least they were human, and I hoped that commonality might at least stand for something.

So I ran into the darkness hoping it would consume me; envelop me and hide me from the monster that fought to be freed.

The demons of Darkdale became angels when the devil was on my tail.

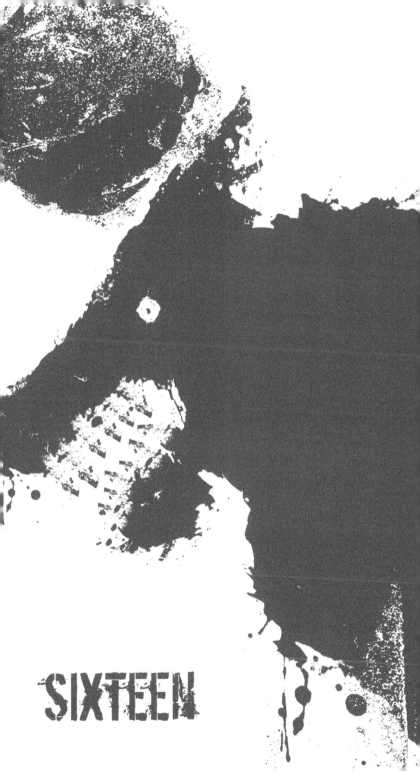

SIXTEEN

Sergeant Kate Shaw (Firearms Officer): Hawkins and I led the way, with Mew and Harrington checking the rear. The prison was dark, with long shadows being cast from the searchlights outside. The place was a mess. Tables overturned, noticeboards pulled from the walls, fire extinguishers cracked open. And the blood. There'd certainly been a lot of infighting, not just with the guards it seemed.

Constable Richard Hoskins (Firearms Officer): All we could do was sit outside and keep the prisoners contained. Some were already losing their bottle and clambered over the barricades to give themselves up. But it was only a handful. Not enough.

I was covering the medics as they pulled dead bodies and survivors from the trashed fire escape. Sergeant Shaw and a few of her team where inside Darkdale. We could do nothing to help. Our orders were to hold the perimeter. To sit outside and wait.

It was then we heard the media show up.

Peter Ball (Prison Guard): It's always a fucking circus when the news reporters storm their way in. We did our best to hold them off. An exclusion zone was set up, but they did all they could to get through. We were suddenly fighting people from both sides. Christ, they made the prisoners look civilised as they demanded *the truth*.

Inspector Thompson called for a press conference. It was a stalling tactic. A bone for the newshounds to maul whilst we got on with the real work.

Sergeant Kate Shaw: We were so close to the roof we could hear them above us, pulling up the tiles and screaming at our colleagues on the ground. I knew very well what would happen if we were discovered. They'd pull us to pieces given the chance.

Our original plan was to storm the place. Hit them hard with a bit of shock and awe and quell the troubles quickly. With our numbers depleted we had to change tact. Check the hostage situation, look for weaknesses, count numbers and find an exit point. It was all about gathering intelligence.

Jorge Wiles (Prisoner): I'd given up on my search for Jimmy. I started checking the bodies that lay on the floor. My thoughts had turned for the worst.

Constable Richard Hoskins: All of a sudden they disappeared. The crowds on the roof vanished back inside. I knew my superiors had seen it, but I radioed the movement in anyway. Something about it gave me a bad feeling.

Jimmy Eades (Prisoner): It was coming. I didn't look back, but I could feel it. I could feel *him*. Mad Dog Mooney was out.

Sergeant Kate Shaw: We'd been lucky so far. The corridors had been quiet. Empty. I wasn't getting cocky, exactly, but I was beginning to think we had a bit of fortune on our side.

Peter Ball: Both the Inspector and the Governor made an appearance for the cameras and newspapers. They didn't really have much choice. As the leading superiors on the scene, it was their call on what information to release.

Sergeant Kate Shaw: Hawkins led the way as we ran across the landing. We could hear voices getting louder on the stairwell below us, then all of a sudden I heard a scream.

I turned back and saw Mew on the floor. Blood was pouring from her left shoulder through a huge hole that had been punctured in her armour. A scaffolding pole lay across her; one end splattered with her blood. She reached out to me and I could see the agony on her face that she tried her best to conceal. It took a moment to understand what had happened, but they were already on us. There was no time to react.

Another pole fell from above and bounced off her visor, knocking Mew's headgear into her face as it smashed onto the protective Perspex, obliterating her nose. Then came another, smacking into her gut; crushing her riot gear and ripping through her stomach.

Peter Ball: I don't know exactly what happened in that press conference, I stayed away from all the media coverage. I knew it would only make me angry. But from all accounts, they wanted blood.

Sergeant Kate Shaw: I turned to face the ceiling, suddenly lit up with torches. Men stood above us, balancing on the metallic mesh overhead. They were aiming scaffolding poles through the gaps in the chains and launching them at us like spears.

I tried to dive out of the way, but one caught my leg. My knee was in agony, but I rolled to the wall in an attempt to find cover. Harrington was hit across the neck. The steel pole smashed his shoulder and knocked him to the ground, rendering him unconscious. I aimed my gun towards them, and although I got off a number of shots, I was wild in my aim. I couldn't prevent the next attack. It snapped his neck as Harrington bled out on the floor.

Constable Richard Hoskins: Gunshots rang out from inside Darkdale. With the press conference starting you couldn't have asked for worse timing.

Sergeant Kate Shaw: Hawkins was cowering on the other side of the landing trying to evade the onslaught of poles. Short controlled bursts were beginning to thin the attackers, but a lucky shot from one of the prisoners struck his trigger hand. He howled as it fractured the bones through his glove.

Above us a man stalked the mesh, watching the other's like they were his army. I aimed my Heckler and Koch straight at his head. If you want to take an army down, first take their leader. He's spouting some kind of Shakespeare babble at us.

"The woman of war, we will sacrifice her." Something like that.

Jimmy Eades: "The fire-eyed maid of smoky war,
All hot and bleeding will we offer them."
It's from Henry IV.

Constable Richard Hoskins: With the windows smashed in we brought out the tear gas. Whatever was happening in there, our guys and gals needed help.

Jimmy Eades: I'm following the noise. Anywhere is safer than with that monster. The more people the better. By the time I reach them, Mark Webster is conducting his army like they're an orchestra. He's relishing in the drama.

Sergeant Kate Shaw: He's absolutely crazy, walking the mesh without a care. Frustratingly I can't get a shot on target.

Constable Richard Hoskins: We get the okay. Tear gas is to be deployed.

Peter Ball: The press and public demanded action be taken, even if it was against our better judgement. The power of the people steamrollered it through. Both the Inspector and the Governor knew the importance of public opinion. I guess their line of thinking was, "It's already a shit storm, it can't get much worse." They couldn't have been more wrong.

Jimmy Eades: I burst in, screaming and hollering. Everyone stops and looks at me. I'm panting and smeared in blood. Even the pinned cops below us stop and stare.

They all pause for a moment and turn to me. My voice isn't loud, yet somehow it carries. They all hear my words.

"It's coming."

Sergeant Kate Shaw: The sound of something metal hitting the ground fills the sudden silence, then a hissing sound. I instantly know what it is and try to cover my face.

Jimmy Eades: Tear gas starts to fill the room. At first I think it's smoke, and a memory of Mr Creevy's burning warehouse flashes through my mind. Then a growl comes from behind me.

Sergeant Kate Shaw: Suddenly there's screams and shouting through the mist. Blood starts raining down on me and Hawkins. There's a roar, like they've got a lion up there with them.

Jimmy Eades: I dive to the side as I feel the monster behind me. Cowering in the corner I watch as it sets upon the others. For a moment they are all in shock at the sight before them, but as the creature launches at the closest prisoner and tears into his neck they all find their feet again.

Some try to fight back, to save their friend, but it's a foolish move.

The tear gas starts to cloud my vision, but Mad Dog seems unaffected. Dark silhouettes collide in the mist amidst cries of agony.

Sergeant Kate Shaw: I get to Hawkins and check he's okay. We need to get down, away from the tear gas before it reaches us in effective quantities. With all the commotion I didn't hear the helicopter blades above the prison.

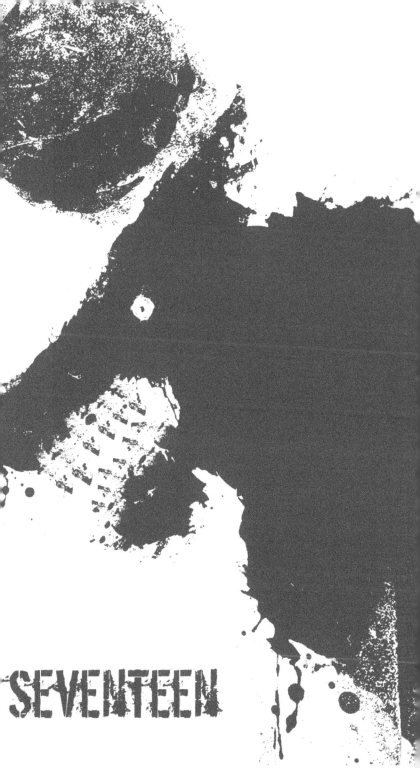

SEVENTEEN

Peter Ball (Prison Guard): No sooner had the press conference ended than the helicopters were called for. Governor Peel was red-faced as he left the meeting. He looked angry; real angry.

Michael Allington (Helicopter Pilot, Police Air Support): We should have told them to stick it. I've never flown in such bad conditions before or since. But when you're new you just follow orders, don't you?

Jimmy Eades (Prisoner): I got to my feet and ran. I think I might have subconsciously followed the sound of the helicopters, but it wasn't something I noted at the time. I just wanted to get clear of the tear gas and away from the slaughter.

My closest unblocked route took me up a set a stairs and before I knew it I was on the roof. The wind almost took me sideways but I steadied myself and took a lungful of clean air. There were others on the roof too.

And through the rain I could see two sets of lights heading towards us.

I crawled across the slippery tiles and watched the choppers hover over head.

Michael Allington: I could hear the arguments over the radio. Bird One was piloted by David Huggins. Good guy too. He knew his stuff which is why he was arguing with the command to drop the ropes.

Peter Ball: We'd launched the tear gas to cause disruption. Provide cover. Next we were going to send in another strike unit. Drop them from the air. Level by level they'd clear the decks; mop up this sorry scum.

The public had spoken and they didn't care much for a rioting population of prisoners.

Michael Allington: In the end Dave's protests were futile. He had no choice but to hold position over the roof and send the team in. Orders are orders. You can't fight the white.

Jimmy Eades: The guys are hurling tiles in the air, but the choppers are too high. Ropes come down from the nearest one, dangling above our heads. Some try to grab hold and pull the chopper down, but they just can't reach. I shout out to the other inmates, attempting to warn them about the monster, but they can't hear over the wind and the sound of the helicopter blades. There's another commotion behind me so I turn back to see what's going on.

A wave of nausea washes through my body. Maybe it

was the adrenalin, I'm not sure. Whatever it was I feel like I'm about to pass out as I see a huge figure climb onto the slates.

Those glowing eyes set into a hulking silhouette.

Constable Richard Hoskins (Firearms Officer): One helicopter's keeping its distance, shining a spot onto the roof. The other is hovering over the prison. The wind is smashing it left and right, but somehow the pilot is holding it together, fighting against the elements and keeping it stable.

Michael Allington: That Huggins was a fantastic pilot. To keep himself in position against that kind of force was something else. I know a lot has been said about him afterwards, but mark my words: he didn't put a foot wrong.

Constable Richard Hoskins: The lights on the helicopters went off as the strike force took to the ropes. After that, I couldn't see shit.

Michael Allington: It's standard practice to turn off the spots. If they're left on, the team's eyes will get used to the light and their pupils will contract. The moment they hit the ground and drop into the darkness they aren't going to be able to see diddly-squat.

Jimmy Eades: Mad Dog leaps into the air and manages to take hold of one of the ropes. The helicopter banks sharply with the sudden shift in weight, but corrects itself. The creature scales the rope with lightning speed and is on the abseiling officer in next to no time. Trapped on the flailing line, he must have been horrified to see that grinning mouth full of teeth and those devilish eyes suddenly appear inches from his own face.

I watched him try to kick out, struggling on the rope as he tried to fend off his attacker, but Mad Dog was far too strong. As the rain lashed down I watched the monster plunge its claws deep into the officer's gut.

Michael Allington: Gunshots start blasting out from the sky. The cop on the opposite rope is freaking out, shooting wildly trying to save his colleague.

Peter Ball: The crowd down below start screaming and running in all directions, panicked they're going to get caught up in this. Suddenly they realise the danger of the situation. About bloody time.

Jimmy Eades: I watch the cop's severed arm fall from a height and thud onto the roof. I'm staring at this limb, shocked at how much blood is draining out, when I hear more shots. I can make out Mooney climbing all over the poor fuck. He bends the guy's head back and sinks those long teeth into his neck. I can literally see an arc of blood squirt into the air as the monster bites at him again and again.

Michael Allington: Then all the cops on Bird One are suddenly going crazy. Not only is there the one on the other rope firing at will, but he's joined by two more inside the chopper.

MAD DOG

Jimmy Eades: The cop's head rolls back and doesn't stop. Savaged from his body, it drops through the air and thuds in an explosion of dark red.

Michael Allington: The bullets are flying, and one hits our side. A second one catches the windscreen. It pings off, but not before leaving a crack down the front. I had no choice. It wasn't desertion. It was survival. Pure and simple.

Jimmy Eades: The monster looks across to the other rope and leaps between them, landing a claw on the police officer and gripping hold, tight. The helicopter starts to sway and back and forth. The pilot loses control as it tilts and lowers, heading towards the prison.

I hit the deck as the chopper swoops, turning to its side in an attempt to halt its descent. I stop my mindless voyeurism and run back to the relative safety of inside, as the chopper banks sharply again and its blades spark against the roof, careering through a crowd and dicing them like mincemeat.

Ducking back inside, I'm thankful the tear gas has mostly cleared, and I'm already on the second floor when I hear the ceiling give way.

Constable Richard Hoskins: The next thing we know the sky lights up with a huge fireball.

Jimmy Eades: Stupidly, I stop to look up. I have a vague memory, a flash of a piece of mortar coming towards me. It must have knocked me out cold.

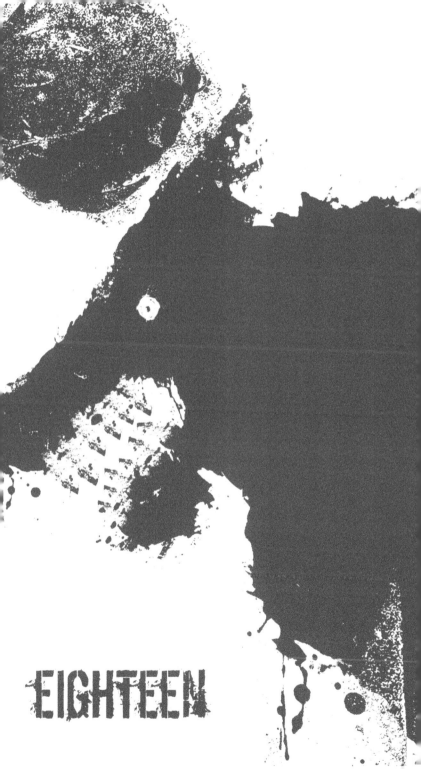

EIGHTEEN

Constable Richard Hoskins (Firearms Officer):
There was a moment of deathly silence. An unnerving
hush, straight after the crash. Everybody was stunned.
No one knew what to do.

Jorge Wiles (Prisoner): We didn't even dare turn our
torches on. The darkness felt safe. We needed to hide.

Peter Ball (Prison Guard): Fire engines lined the
street, but there was no way in. They even tried
appealing to the prisoners inside to help. Calling through
megaphones. But that just fell on deaf ears. Scumbags.

Jorge Wiles: People were turning on each other left,
right and centre. With the nonces and guards all
barbarically tortured to death, and their leader missing,
the general populace of Darkdale prison were lost;
lashing out at each other for no good reason.

Peter Ball: Paramedics were running all over the place trying their best to deal with the idiots that had been hit by falling shrapnel. Public, press. Kind of serves them right for being too close. Except for Governor Peel. No one deserved that.

Jorge Wiles: The helicopter had torn a hole right through the roof, pulling down walls and walkways as it crashed straight through to the ground floor. The fallen debris had blocked all passageways that weren't already buried behind make-shift barricades. There was no way out.

We could hear the pleas from outside calling through megaphones to let them in, but we had no way of responding. Or helping.

Peter Ball: I was taken to identify the body, and when I arrived he was still stood upright. Two cops were doing their best to dislodge the helicopter's rotary blade from the dirt it had imbedded itself in. The blade had sliced clean through Governor Peel's head and chest, straight down the middle, then stuck into the ground behind him, preventing his corpse from dropping to the floor. His grimace was lopsided as the two sides of his face slowly slid away from each other. It almost looked like he was smiling.

Jorge Wiles: I can't believe Jimmy survived. Crazy bastard. I pulled him out of the wreckage of the downed helicopter. Bits of chopper were strewn all over the prison after that thing came crashing through the ceiling. Jimmy had a nasty cut across his head that was swelling up, but other than that he looked fine. Absolutely crazy bastard.

Jimmy Eades (Prisoner): I woke up with a strange taste in my mouth.

Jorge Wiles: We were hiding out in the guard's mess. I'd dragged Jimmy to our hiding place and fed him a beaker of water, hoping to revive him. The kitchens had been torn out in the riot and somewhere gas was spewing. We couldn't find the source in the dark and turning on a light was a bad idea.

We had no choice but to grin and bear it. Put up with the stink and the foul aftertaste every time we took a deep breath. But we were thankful for the dark.

At least the darkness felt safe.

Jimmy Eades: I look around trying to make sense of what had just happened and how I'd got here. Jorge is stood over me with a drink in his hands. He places the edge of the cup to my lips. I don't recognise the others, they are covered in a mixture of dust and blood. They looked frightened. Broken.

I remember thinking: *I don't want to be that way. I'm going to survive this.*

I'm going to get home. I'm going to see Hannah.

The water felt good as it slid down my throat, but there was a strange taste; something not quite right about it. My head spun, my thoughts still scrambled. *Was I drinking poison?* That's all that circled round my mind. Looping and looping until the thought grew loud enough to drown out any reason.

I spat it out and pushed the beaker away.

Hannah's face grew clearer, galvanising my will to live, but with thoughts of her came another.

Mooney.

Jorge Wiles: Jimmy started struggling. Even with concussion he was a live wire.

Jimmy Eades: I tried to warn them about Mad Dog. That he was stalking Darkdale. That he was a monster; a werewolf. But they didn't want to hear.

Jorge Wiles: I had a lot of time for that kid but he was off his rocker, and he wouldn't shut up. He was putting us all in danger. Blowing our cover. I'm seconds away from knocking him out, but instead I stand up and walk away. He can fight his own battles. He'd survived this far. He'd already proved he's capable enough. He didn't need me.

What help could I have been anyway? Jimmy was already too far gone.

Jimmy Eades: I push past the hands trying to hold me down, and get to my feet. All I can think about is getting out. Getting clear of Darkdale. So before they can catch me again, I'm running away from their hideout.

To be honest I don't really know what I'm doing.

Run, just run, is all I'm thinking.

I'm hardly fifty metres away from the others when I catch sight of a familiar face in the wreck of the helicopter. I stop as he looks up at me.

"Like the bad penny," he sneers as I watch him

struggle to breathe.

His arm is trapped under a pile of rubble and there's a metal support coming out through the side of his chest. He's spitting blood as he forces a smile.

"You want that sweetheart of yours to live? You'd better give me a hand," he threatens.

I think back to Hannah again and a strange cocktail of joy and grief floods my mind. My stomach grows light. I can't tell if I'm scared or excited.

I've got to end this, I'm thinking. I've got to end this, now.

Jorge Wiles: The kid was crazier than I thought. He's a danger to himself and everyone else. I wasn't going back out there. Not then. He was on his own.

Jimmy Eades: A voice calls out behind me.

"Hold it right there!"

It's a woman's voice.

Sergeant Kate Shaw (Firearms Officer): Through the shit and debris we made it to the ground floor. The number of prisoners left inside had dwindled considerably. Those that were left looked lost; angry, but no focus to vent their aggression.

Cleaning them up was an easy job, and one I began to delight in.

Jimmy Eades: Cops. I see the woman and her colleague, a man; their guns trained on me. They have no interest in my arrest. They want out as much as the rest of us. I'm nothing more than an obstacle to their freedom. I'm as good as dead.

Sergeant Kate Shaw: He's standing by the wreckage with a look on his face that I can't read. Is he scared? Is he smiling?

Jimmy Eades: I see something move in the low light to the side of them. A pair of eyes glint in the darkness, their colours mismatched from the scar that runs down his face.

Sergeant Kate Shaw: Without warning he's on us. My gun is knocked clear from my hand, and as I scrabble to reach it I hear Hawkins shrieking like nothing I've ever heard.

Jimmy Eades: Mooney knocks the man to the ground and slashes through his body armour with ease. The cop is thrashing around under the monster's weight. Legs and arms flailing, trying to knock the creature over. But it's too heavy. Too strong.

Blood is pouring from the man's chest as Mad Dog is tearing into his flesh. I watch, transfixed, as his screams get louder. Every second his chest is opening up more. Meat is clawed away to reveal ribs. I can see the rapid rise and fall of his lungs; the inflating membranes exposed to the very air they breathe. A large, gelatinous sack falls from his torso. I realise it's his stomach.

Another slash rips his throat open, muting his screams. The next one tears out his windpipe. The next and I can see the bones of his neck.

I want to throw up.

Sergeant Kate Shaw: I don't have time to find my gun in the mess of metal and rubble, so I pull out my knife. Yeah, it's not standard issue, but I like to keep it around. It's not the first time it's saved my life.

Jimmy Eades: The woman dives at the monster and thrusts a knife into his shoulder. She knocks him from her colleague, but even from this distance I can tell it's too late. The guy's long gone.

The police woman gets to her feet, but she's lost him in the dark. I keep watching. I'm insignificant here. This sport doesn't involve me; not right now. These two players are in a different league.

Sergeant Kate Shaw: He felt like he was made of stone. My shoulder's still aching from the impact, and now I've lost my knife. My weapon is stuck in his shoulder. I'm searching in the gloom, trying to listen out for a signal; some kind of tell-tale alert to his location.

As I'm doing that, I'm manically searching my pouches and pockets. Searching for something to defend myself with. My fingers brush against a lighter and I instinctively clutch it; holding it out like a sword.

I'm thinking, *maybe I'll burn the bastard.*

Jimmy Eades: A deep growl bounces off the walls. I'm trying to work out the direction of the sound, when all of a sudden I see a flash of his huge teeth as he launches towards the cop. She doesn't stand a hope in hell, and although she makes a valiant attempt to dodge, she is knocked to the ground, dropping her lighter.

Mooney stands above her, towering over her prone body. I think about Hannah. I wonder if this is what she looked like when he lay his bestial wrath on her.

I glance across to Mark Webster. He is in shock, but his wounds don't look life-threatening. I'm sure he'll pull through. My feet are wet, and looking down I see I am stood in a large puddle. It stinks of diesel. Aviation fuel from the helicopter. I step away from the liquid and kneel down, picking up the cop's dropped lighter.

Sergeant Kate Shaw: Fuck knows how I survived. I was out cold. Some of us are born lucky I guess.

Jimmy Eades: I remember smiling, thinking back to my revenge on my old boss, Jonathan Creevy. How I snuck back to his warehouse late at night, doused some crates in petrol and watched the place burn. I didn't realise Mr Creevy was working late. I wasn't to know he'd get caught in the blaze and die at my hands. Maybe it was karma that sent those burning embers flying into my face, but I didn't escape there unscathed either.

I scratched at my old wound as I was reminded of it. I always did when I was nervous.

I didn't know I had killed Mr Creevy, but at that moment, in Darkdale, I am very aware of what I am about to do.

I flick the wheel and see the flint spark. A flame dances from the top of the lighter.

My grin widens. I remember the smell when I awoke in the guard's mess. The smell of gas.

The puddle of diesel is bigger than I thought, running off in all directions. I look at the grimacing face of Mark

Webster. I watch Mooney, the werewolf, lower himself on the policewoman, and slowly I place the flame against the fuel.

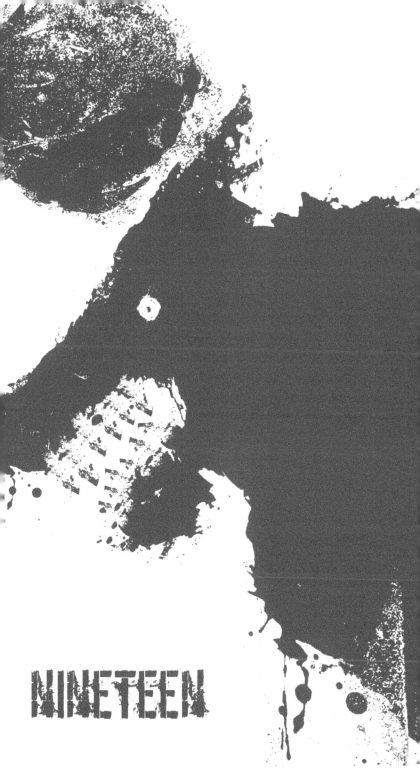

NINETEEN

Jimmy Eades (Prisoner): The beauty of the flames mesmerise me for a moment as they snake up the twisting stream of fuel, but I quickly snap out of it and turn away. I'm heading up a flight of steps when I hear a boom as the flames reach the gas.

Constable Richard Hoskins (Firearms Officer): Suddenly we're all cowering. A huge explosion rips through the prison. If people were panicked before, then I don't know what happened after that. Hysteria. Maybe that's the word.

Peter Ball (Prison Guard): People were fleeing the scene, frightened this was some kind of terrorist assault.

Jimmy Eades: The next thing I know I'm two floors up. My ears are ringing and I'm spitting out blood. My nose is clogged with the smell of burnt hair, and after touching my head I realise why.

The world is twisting. Spinning. I stumble to my feet and it takes me a while to gain proper balance. But that doesn't stop me from surging forward.

Everybody else is dead, or so I thought, but I'm still trapped in this hell hole. My survival instincts push me onward, urging me to find an escape. Fire is raging below so I go in the only direction I can. I keep going up.

Peter Ball: Smoke is billowing out the windows. My eyes are streaming. I can hardly see.

The North Tower is still standing; fuck knows how.

Constable Richard Hoskins: The heat. The smoke. It's driving us all back. No one can get close.

Jimmy Eades: I clamber up onto the roof for the second time that night. My hands tingle, but somehow I don't feel the cold as I crawl over the wet roof tiles and shakily get to my feet. There's smoke spewing from the fire, making it a nightmare for me to see.

I know it's too high for me to jump off the edge of the building, but the North Tower offers me some hope. If I can make my way over to it, I've got a chance of climbing down the scaffolding and reaching safety.

Of course that's easier said than done. The sloped surface of the roof is slippery from the rain and the thick smoke is getting in my eyes. The next thing I know I've lost my balance and my feet have flown out from under me.

I hit the deck and tumble down the roof, my face scraping across the rough clay. I reach out and try to stop myself, but it feels like I'm grasping at seaweed. My fingers find a gap in the tiles, and not a moment too soon. By the time my arms tense and halt my fall, my feet are dangling off the edge.

I pull myself back up and glance down at the surrounding crowds. The sight of the sheer drop makes my stomach flip. I turn back, determined to keep my vision looking up, not down; and that's when I see it.

A few metres away, and splayed out in a crumpled mess, is the werewolf. I stop breathing for a moment and keep my attention fixed on the monster. His hair is burnt, with patches of scalded, bare skin, but I can see his chest slowly rise and fall. The bastard's still alive!

I wipe blood from my chin and slowly, carefully, crawl back to the peak of the roof, doing my best not to wake the beast. Part of me wants to crawl over to Mooney, to roll him over and drop him from this height, but I'm too frightened he'll wake up.

Peter Ball: The fire service take charge. It's now officially a disaster zone and they're calling the shots.

Constable Richard Hoskins: The goggles may have protected my eyes, but the smell and stench: it was foul. We remained steadfast and kept our positions as we covered the fire crew. They took axes to the doors of Darkdale, trying to force their way through the barricades.

Jimmy Eades: I reach the North Tower and slowly ease my weight onto the turret, thankful that the smoke isn't as thick where I'm stood. The wind is trying its hardest to force me off, and I don't know whether it's concussion or vertigo, but the whole structure seems to be swaying in the storm.

I look back and the monster's still lying on its side.

Constable Richard Hoskins: The fire was growing. You could see it through the windows. This orange glow spreading further and further up the floors.

Jimmy Eades: It looks an even bigger drop from the tower than it did the main prison. There isn't much left of the scaffolding; the rioters saw to that. But there is still enough left for my plan to work. There's still enough of a connecting structure to climb down.

I grasp the poles, but my hands instantly slide off. I didn't realise metal could be so frictionless when wet. There was no way I could get any kind of grip. I needed another plan.

Constable Richard Hoskins: The hoses came on, and they aimed them right over the prison. It was impressive to see the arc of water reach so high. Rain alone wasn't going to stop that fire.

Jimmy Eades: I heard a patter, much heavier than the rain on the roof. At first I thought Mooney had woken, but turning around I watched a jet of water dissipate over the prison. It took me a while to work out it was coming from a fire engine's hose.

The water splashes everywhere, and it's not long before I'm watching the monster stir as the spray hits his face.

I step backwards, just stopping my foot from slipping off as I realise I'm right on the edge of the tower. Mad Dog climbs to his feet and catches sight of me. I consider throwing myself down the scaffolding, sliding down it like a fireman's pole. But it's not one straight run and without the grip I know I'd fall clear of it within minutes. I'd end up burger meat on the ground.

I edge forward to get better footing and be clear of the drop, but by the time I look back up, the werewolf is charging towards me. A swipe from his claw easily slices open my arm, and despite all my other injuries, this one stings the greatest. Its pain steals my breath and my legs want to collapse from under me.

Scooping up a loose roof tile I throw it at the monster. Mad Dog shields his head as the tile connects. Using the distraction I pick up a discarded pole and cumbersomely swing it towards him. He dodges my attack and the momentum of the weapon carries me round, the weight of the metal pole pulling itself from my hands as my strength fades. An excruciating pain tears down my back as Mooney strikes again.

I right myself and watch the creature run towards me once more. My foot slips on the edge of the tower, but I correct it and prevent myself from falling. The werewolf leaps; his claws aimed at me and his lips curled back, ready to sink his canine teeth deep into my flesh.

At the last minute I duck and he flies over the top of me.

There's only one way he could have gone, and that's over the edge.

Constable Richard Hoskins: The smoke thins a little

as the fire begins to recede.

Jimmy Eades: I pick up the loose pole I'd dropped earlier and head towards the end of the tower, holding it like an over-sized spear. I've seen enough films to know the bastard might still be holding on just below. So until I've checked it out, I refuse to relax from the threat.

But as I smashed into the aging tiles and hurtled down through the roof I didn't realise just how quick he would be; launching at me and striking out as soon as I got close to the edge.

I had no chance. Thrown backwards with this man-animal on top of me, snarling in anger, we both went crashing through the roof and into the North Tower.

Constable Richard Hoskins: Finally we get a good view of Darkdale again, and the damage done to it. The building is a crumbling mess. The firemen are still digging their way through the barricades, but I remember thinking, *What's the point? No one's survived that.*

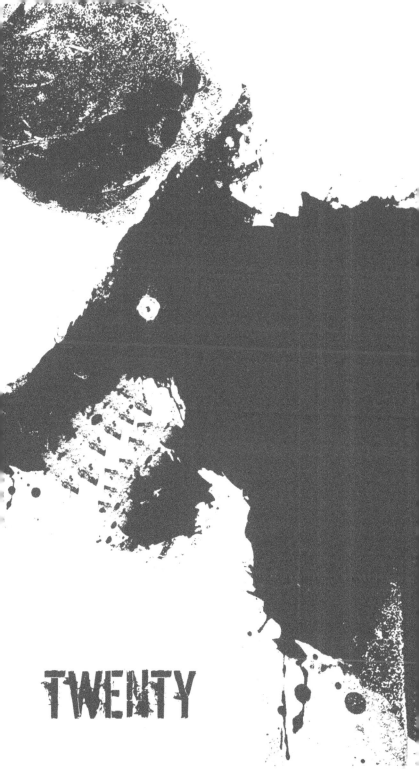

TWENTY

Jimmy Eades (Prisoner): I must have crashed through a few floors before I finally stopped. My back felt like it was in pieces, and if it hadn't been for the adrenaline suppressing the pain, I don't think I'd have been able to stand.

Groggy from the fall, I got to my feet as quickly as I could, expecting to fend off another attack. But Mooney had vanished. I looked around, hurriedly, first for my attacker and secondly for a way out, all the while trying to make some sense of where I was. The walls were black and charred, blistered from some previous blaze. The floor was in no better condition.

No wonder I'd fallen through it so easily; the place had been burnt to a cinder.

Charcoaled remains of furniture lay strewn around the room. Symbols had been sprayed onto the walls, crude notes from the builders and architects as they'd marked up what was structurally sound and what wasn't. I precariously stepped forward and heard the floor beneath me groan and crumble as it tried to hold my weight. With extra care, I made my way on tiptoe for fear of another fall.

The place looked familiar to me, but I couldn't say why. I stopped at the remains of a desk. Blistered as it was, I recognised its leather-topped surface. There was a metal nameplate, part blackened, but half readable. My memory filled in the blanks: Dr G Anderson.

I pulled at the drawers and the wood crumbled around the lock, but there was little inside to sate my curiosity.

I couldn't quite put my finger on it. I'd seen this place before, but where? Everything seemed to invoke a memory, one that failed to pull itself from the mire of my subconscious with any form of clarity.

I wrenched open another drawer, this time finding a pile of paper, browned from the heat of the blaze, but largely undamaged due to the protection of the desk.

Again I saw the name: Dr George Anderson. This meant something to me. Triggered another memory, but again one I could not grasp.

The papers appeared to be case notes on patients; prisoners. Millard, Jobling, Sholtbolt. These names meant nothing to me. But then something caught my eye. *Mooney.*

My head began to pound and my stomach tightened.

Then something else: *Mad Dog.*

The Websters.

I leant against the rickety desk as I began to grow faint.

James Eades.

A creaking came from upstairs; the sound of

movement above me. My senses sharpened and I abandoned my search for answers, hastily heading downstairs to find an exit.

It immediately felt cooler as I stepped onto the ground floor. The wind was whipping through the broken glass and between the bars that lined the windows, helping to clear the sweat from my forehead.

Lights from the emergency vehicles flashing outside illuminated the room in a rhythmic blue strobe. It reduced my vision from snatches of clarity to complete darkness, alternating every few seconds.

As I move through the room I am half guessing, forced to fill in the blanks when the darkness shrouds all. My brain does a pretty good job at piecing together the scraps of information my eyes feed it, and I make out the fact that the builders had already started work down here; tools and machinery were stored against the far wall and the whole floor had been gutted, leaving an empty, echoing expanse.

Two skips were full to the brim with masonry and piping. A forklift truck stood at the back, and I couldn't help but think back to my old job in the warehouse; of all those plans I'd made with Hannah. Of working hard and earning money so I could help put her through University and create a future together.

That felt like a lifetime ago.

There's a noise in the dark and I know it's coming for me. The padding of its paws grow clearer. I run to the door, but it's locked. I kick and punch, but it's not budging, and the monster's getting closer.

Running back to one of the skips, I pull out a length of pipe and hold it up, ready to attack. My back's against the wall and I'm scanning the area. The room is flashing from the lights of the emergency vehicles outside. The strobe is messing with my eyes, making it hard to focus. I see a movement from the staircase as the monster crawls down the steps, taken to walking on all fours as it stalks in the darkness.

I catch snatches of its unnatural image as it dismounts the staircase and turns its head to face me. In a display of power it opens its mouth, showing off its sabre-like teeth with a low growl, even more threatening for its controlled restraint.

It picks up pace, and I've nowhere left to run as it gallops towards me; no plans to defeat it. All I've got is this crummy metal pipe. Just hit and hope.

I swing as the monster launches itself towards me. My weapon folds like tin foil against the creature's side and does little to stop its attack. The bastard knocks me to the floor then grabs me by the throat. It stands on two legs and lifts me up, holding me at eye level with those weird refracting eyes. They look bigger as they stare at me. Its teeth seem longer. Sharper.

I don't know what to do. I struggle in its grip, but there's no loosening its hold. I reach in to my pockets and curse myself for losing that lighter.

The monster pulls me closer. Its hot breath warms my neck as it opens its mouth wider.

My fingers catch hold of something in one of my trouser pockets. The smooth metallic surface was so familiar to my touch. It was the pen I'd been given; a present from Father Matthews.

I pull it out and thrust it towards Mooney.

It catches the monster, and I drive it, deep into its

eye.

A roar of pain echoes in the tower as its claw releases its grip on me and I fall to the floor. Turning, I run to the forklift truck. To my delight there's a driver's card left on the seat. I insert it and start the engine up. My mind is racing as I try to remember my training. I check the lever and switch it to forward. The monster is already shaking off the pain, so I stamp my foot on the pedal and hope there's enough distance to pick up speed.

Pulling at the other lever, I raise the forks to mid-way. Mooney looks at me, but doesn't have a chance to do anything about it. By the time that son-of-a-bitch knows what's going on I've already collided with him. The forks crack into his ribs; my momentum keeping him pinned to the vehicle.

Those eyes look at me, a mixture of anger and sadness. I smile back at the bastard. I got the fucker now.

I aim towards the wall and smash into it. The forklift smacks a hole through the other side, forcing the monster through the bricks. I fall out of my seat as the vehicle rides up on a pile of rubble and up-ends, tumbling onto its side.

I recognise the room as I stand above Mooney's crushed and mangled body. A chair stands in the middle with broken straps. Blood is smeared across the floor and ceiling. Through the door is a corridor strewn with corpses. A bloodied and torn lab coat lies scrunched up in the corner. It's Mooney's cell!

I crouch down beside him, no longer afraid. His face looks less animal as his laboured breathing begins to slow, and by the time his chest stops still I see nothing more than a pathetic man, scared and desperate.

The emergency services have the blaze under the control.

The fires of hell were fading.

The devil lay at my feet.

Dying.

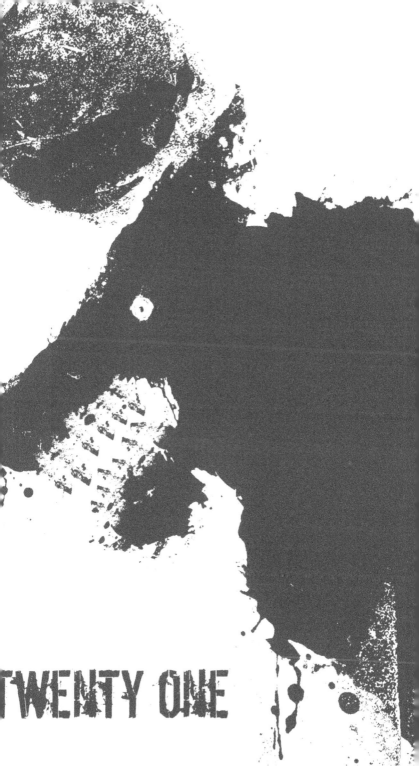

TWENTY ONE

Peter Ball (Prison Guard): Of course everything came out during the inquiry that took place in the aftermath.

Jorge Wiles (Prisoner): Everyone tells it differently. No two stories are every exactly the same. The inquiry got as best a handle on it as they could, but people were reluctant to talk.

Peter Ball: It was a disaster that should have been avoided, and everyone was protecting their own backs. It could have been completely mitigated if it wasn't for some really stupid mistakes.

Looking back, the generator was on its last legs. It was only a matter of time before it broke down. We'd overused it, hoping it would last until the next financial year when a new budget was granted. It was only meant to be a backup. It wasn't designed to be run continuously. Hindsight is a wonderful thing... and that goes for all matters regarding this sorry mess.

Jorge Wiles: I'm lucky to be talking to you right now. Not everyone that night had my good fortune.

Peter Ball: There was a lot of people questioning why he was taken back into Darkdale in the first place. I guess if the true events had been released about the first incident, about the real reason for the fire in the North Tower and his subsequent escape, this second disaster might not ever have happened.

From the notes of Dr Anderson (Former Prison Doctor): James Eades is a severely troubled individual.

Father Matthews (Prison Chaplain): By the time someone got a message to me and I arrived at the prison the fire crew had already gained access. I felt awful, at home peacefully snoozing whilst all this had taken place. I know it sounds irrational but I felt like, if I had have been there, I could have helped in some way.

Peter Ball: Where else would they put him? We all figured lightning wouldn't strike twice. But truth be told we were still crippled from his first assault. Somehow the blame was aimed at George Anderson. They said he failed the prisoner, and the prison. Easy to blame the dead. He was nothing more than a scapegoat. The doctor did his absolute best for Jimmy. His replacement, Dr Edwards, she just wanted to prod him and record what he said. Send him fake letters from his lover and watch the reaction. Try and make a name for herself in psychiatry.

Jorge Wiles: Dr Edwards was a junkie. Always getting high on her own supply. She didn't deserve what ultimately happened to her, but rumours are she was sent here with her tail between her legs; disgraced from her previous practice after suspicions of morphine abuse.

She meant well, I have no doubt, but she had her own demons to slay. If you're messed up in your own mind how are you supposed to help someone else?

Constable Richard Hoskins (Firearms Officer): With the blaze under control we escorted the fire service in, but we needn't have bothered. The prisoners were nothing more that dust covered ghosts. They came out with their hands up; placid and co-operative.

From the notes of Dr Edwards (Prison Doctor): Despite his talk of the Websters I have not been able to find any record of a prisoner in Darkdale with the same name.

Jorge Wiles: Only Websters in Darkdale was that damned dictionary. And Jimmy soon put an end to that one.

From the notes of Dr Anderson: His delusions are growing stronger, manifesting themselves into distinct personalities.

He tells me stories. I am having trouble deciphering what is fact and what is not. James has a strong imagination and a persuasive conviction to pass tall tales off as truth.

Peter Ball: How many times do you have to hear it? The Websters did not exist. They were just some fucked up thing inside his head.

From the notes of Dr Anderson: At times he talks of his own actions belonging to another; watching them from afar as if he's watching a different person entirely. Other times he goes off on complete flights of fantasy, embellishing the truth and describing events that simply did not happen.

Jorge Wiles: Jimmy could never remember his first stay in prison. Before he escaped. I don't pretend to understand why, and never talked to him about it. I didn't like to push it.

From the notes of Dr Anderson: I am unable to ascertain whether he knows he is lying, or truly believes these fantasies.

Craig Creevy (Son of Mr Jonathan Creevy): He tell you it was an accident that my dad died in that warehouse fire? You checked the police report on that one? And his sentence?

Evidence shows my dad was beaten and tied to a chair prior to the warehouse going up. That wasn't an accident. Jimmy's a fucking murderer, plain and simple.

Oh sorry, not Jimmy, what are they calling him now, Mad Dog? Yeah, that's right.

Jorge Wiles: Jimmy was sent down for murder and arson. In his first short visit he strangled Dr Anderson with his own belt, watched his fellow inmates burn as he set the North Tower ablaze and in the melee stole a guard's uniform and slipped out into the night. He could be as dangerous as he was cunning.

Peter Ball: Who'd have thought he'd have gone back to his girlfriend after escaping prison? They tell me it's quite common. Lost in a strange world, people seek the comforts they once knew.

We kept his first escape quiet from the press. We didn't want to alarm the public.

Of course when we caught him mauling his ex-lover and cannibalising a little girl, there was no way we could keep a lid on that.

The press had a fucking field day.

From the notes of Dr Anderson: James is growing increasingly interested in a myth; a legend that I've heard often within Darkdale. It concerns a character by the name of Mitch *Mad Dog* Mooney. Researching this character, I found him to be based on fact.

Peter Ball: We thought he'd got lucky the first time; that he was a threat we could keep quelled by the prisoners' own brand of justice. Turns out we underestimated him.

After he murdered his own cellmate, Forbes, he was locked up tight, moved into the isolation cells. After the attack in the canteen he was watched at all times. We should have done that sooner. That was the one thing

Dr Edwards got right.

Jorge Wiles: The doctor allowed me to visit him when he was in Solitary. Those last few days when he wasn't allowed back in the library. Jimmy was a good kid. When he *was* Jimmy.

But when he wasn't... well, you know the damage he caused.

From the notes of Dr Anderson: Mitch Mooney was of Irish descent, originally working for Hamish the Hammer, a notorious gangster in Northern Ireland. Mooney became an enforcer with a fearsome reputation, but one with increasingly strange and erratic behaviour. It is hard to separate fact from fiction, but police reports do suggest some evidence of cannibalism.

This *Mad Dog* was reportedly shot and killed in England, Birmingham whilst doing a job for crime kingpin, Carlito John, but his body was never recovered.

The myth states that he was cursed by a gypsy whilst collecting protection money from a traveller's site and doomed to forever walk the earth in a state of never-ending agony. Even death would not save him from his torment.

His only respite came each full moon, when his pain would be temporarily relinquished.

In return for this momentary relief he had to satisfy the hunger of the demon inside by consuming human flesh.

Inmates talk of this Mad Dog, this legend, like some kind of a boogeyman; a ghost that walks amongst the shadows in the alleyways of our cities, wreaking revenge on those unfaithful to their gangland allegiances.

Of course this is utter nonsense and not a concern in itself, but its dark subject matter is something I wish to steer James away from.

Hannah Miller (University Student): When he got sent down the first time, Jimmy used to call me on the phone from prison. He used to tell me about Mooney, and the monsters inside his head. At first I laughed, thinking it was all a joke, but it quickly grew scary. There was Jimmy, and then there was Mooney. It creeped me out.

I told him it was over.

I never expected to see him again.

In a way I never did.

The next time I saw him, in the alley after he escaped, that wasn't Jimmy.

His hair was long and that god-awful beard. He'd really let himself go. He'd changed. Not just on the outside, but mentally too.

That was Mooney.

That was Mad Dog.

Jorge Wiles: Jimmy. Mooney. It was hard to understand who you were talking to at times.

Father Matthews: I walked through the carnage of this second atrocity and found myself instinctively heading to Solitary. When I got there, there he was, in his cell sat atop a pile of rubble, clutching a bleeding eye: young Jimmy.

I couldn't believe he was still alive. He'd made a lot

of enemies.

Jimmy Eades (Prisoner): I told you, you'd believe.
Monsters exist.
I know.
I am one.

CONTRIBUTORS

J. R. Park

Michael Allington (Helicopter Pilot, Police Air Support) is a helicopter pilot in service with the UK police aviation aerial support.

Dr George Anderson (Former Prison Doctor) is deceased. His children are currently in a court battle to contest his will.

Peter Ball (Prison Guard) has since retired from the prison service and is secretary to the Urban Canal Fishing committee.

Oliver Coleborn (Lawyer) continues to practice law whilst avoiding questions about his legal representative of Jimmy *Mad Dog Mooney* Eades. Despite offers of a book deal from many of the major publishers, Mr Coleborn has maintained his professional discretion.

Craig Creevy (Son of Mr Jonathan Creevy) has since returned from a three week vacation in Las Vegas. He now runs a haulage firm, set up from the insurance pay out of his father's business.

Jimmy Eades (Prisoner) has since had his conviction reassessed and now resides in a top psychiatric hospital for the criminally insane. The exact location of his residence is one that has been kept top secret, despite rumours continuing to surface every few months of another escape. We are contractually bound not to reveal the whereabouts or source of our interview material.

Dr Nicola Edwards (Prison Doctor) is deceased. Her husband, Derrick, is set to remarry in the new year.

Constable Richard Hoskins (Firearms Officer) continues to serve within the police firearms unit and plays, part time, as a guitarist in punk band The New Urinals.

Father Matthews (Prison Chaplain) is awaiting retirement in a year's time and plans to emigrate to Thailand with a stop off in India to 'find himself.'

Hannah Miller (University Student) is on course for 2:1 in her Business Studies degree, despite the setbacks caused from her assault, and currently volunteers at a local kennels.

Sergeant Kate Shaw (Firearms Officer) is tipped for promotion although her recent celebrity status has seen a number of offers to be the face and body of gym brands and work-out routines.

Inspector Geoffrey Thompson (Firearms Officer) has no comment.

Jorge Wiles (Prisoner) has since served his time in prison and makes a living writing pulp thrillers.

ABOUT THE AUTHOR

J. R. Park is an author of horror fiction and co-founder of the Sinister Horror Company. Using pulp horror as his base palate, Park has been ebbing away at the genre's boundaries but never waning with his enthusiasm for the source material.

His first real taste of horror was Michael Jackson's *Thriller* music video, and in turn, An American Werewolf in London; both of which explain why he always wanted to write a werewolf book.

Park's books have received critical praise, most notably with the brutal and intricate Upon Waking, and the slasher homage Punch.

As well as writing, Park also spends time editing, and has been honoured to edit stories by long time heroes Shaun Hutson, Graham Masterton and Guy N Smith.

He currently resides in Bristol, UK.

TERROR BYTE – J. R. PARK

Street tough Detective Norton is a broken man.

Still grieving the murder of his girlfriend he is called to investigate the daylight slaughter of an entire office amid rumours of a mysterious and lethal computer program. As the conspiracy unfolds the technological killer has a new target.
Fighting for survival Norton must also battle his inner demons, the wrath of MI5 and a beautiful but deadly mercenary only known as Orchid.

Unseen, undetectable and unstoppable.
In the age of technology the most deadly weapon is a few lines of code.

TERROR BYTE

J.R. PARK

PUNCH – J. R. PARK

It's carnival night in the seaside town of Stanswick Sands
and tonight blood will stain the beach red.

Punch and Judy man, Martin Powell, returns after ten
years with a dark secret. As his past is revealed Martin
must face the anger of the hostile townsfolk, pushing
him to the very edge of sanity.

Humiliated and stripped of everything he holds dear,
Martin embarks on a campaign of murderous revenge,
seeking to settle scores both old and new.

The police force of this once sleepy town can't react
quick enough as they watch the body count grow at the
hands of a costumed killer.

Can they do enough to halt the malicious mayhem of the
twisted Punch?

PUNCH

J. R. Park

"It's a heartbreaking tale. I'd strongly urge anyone, looking for a straight forward raw read to buy this as soon as possible."
DK Ryan, author of Egor The Rat & creator of HorrorWorlds.com

"Graphical nightmares effectively place the reader in an uneasy position."
Horror Palace

"A rousing combo of parental angst and seething evil. A great spin on the post-modern serial killer."
Daniel Marc Chant, author of Burning House

"A hard hitting story of the darker side of life in a sleepy little seaside town."
Paul Pritchard, Amazon reviewer

195

UPON WAKING – J. R. PARK

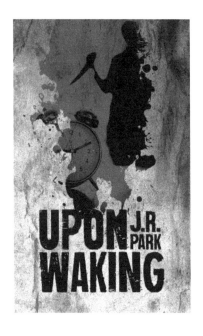

What woke you from your sleep?
Was it the light coming through the curtains? The traffic
from the street outside?

Or was it the scratching through the walls? The cries of
tormented anguish from behind locked doors? The
desperate clawing at the woodwork from a soul hell bent
on escape?

Welcome to a place where the lucky ones die quickly.

Upon waking, the nightmare truly begins.

"Upon Waking is a novel that will challenge you as a reader." – Ginger Nuts of Horror

"An absolute masterclass in gut-wrenchingly violent horror." – DLS Reviews

"J. R. Park has written one of the most painfully twisted books I have ever had the pleasure of reading. I loved it!" – " Book Lovers

"Justin Park needs help. I can't think of any other way of putting it. The part of his mind that this story came from must be one of the darkest places in the universe. His writing however, is just wonderful." – Confessions of a Reviewer

"It's almost like poetry in form and prose. But it's a trick. A fantastically disgusting trick." – Thomas S Flowers, author of Reinhiet

"Seriously – buy this book!" – Matt Shaw, author of Sick B*stards

197

THE EXCHANGE – J. R. PARK

Unemployed and out of ideas, Jake and his friends
head into town for something to do.

But before long they are in over their heads.
Determined to get their friend back from the
clutches of a lethal and shadowy group, the teenagers
find themselves in possession of an object with
mysterious powers.

With their sanity crumbling amidst a warping reality,
the gang are cornered on a wasteland in the middle of
the city, caught in a bloodthirsty battle between criminal
underlords, religious sects and sadistic maniacs.

Nightmares become reality as the stakes begin to rise.
Who will have the upper hand and who will survive this
deadly encounter as they bargain for their lives in this
most deadly exchange.

Amazon reviewer comments:

"The most purely entertaining horror novel I've read this year. And it has unicorns!"

"The Exchange is the stuff of nightmares."

"A thrill ride of suspense, action and mystery."

"It is a real roller-coaster, packing in twists galore; plenty of gore, fascinating theologies and memorable protagonists."

POSTAL – J. R. PARK & MATT SHAW

From Matt Shaw Publications & the Sinister Horror
Company. Two of horror's most warped minds join
forces in one book.

It was a bold move, an initiative by a truly inspirational
leader.

The scheme was a simple one. Each month a letter
would be sent to selected people; thirteen in total.
Within that month the receiver of the letter was given
the lawful right to kill one person. It didn't matter who it
was or how they did it.
The receiver was granted the right to commit murder
with no legal consequences.

The world would never be the same again.

DEATH DREAMS IN A
WHOREHOUSE – J. R. PARK

"This is a frigging superb short story! Think Eli Roth's 'Hostel' meets Edward Lee's 'The Chosen', crossed with a Clive Barker style search for the ultimate sensual thrill. Fast-paced, tightly-written and incredibly atmospheric," wrote DLS reviews about Clandestine Delights, a story featured in this volume.

Death Dreams in a Whorehouse collects nine blood-soaked tales of terror and intrigue from the mind of J. R. Park; a mind that Scream magazine described as 'one of the darkest places in the universe'.

Containing the stories Treats, Mandrill, Connors, Clandestine Delights, Head Spin, The Svalbard Horror, Screams In The Night, The Festering Death and I Love You.

For up to date information on the work of J. R. Park visit:

JRPark.co.uk
Facebook.com/JRParkAuthor
Twitter @Mr_JRPark

For further information on the Sinister Horror Company visit:

SinisterHorrorCompany.com
Facebook.com/sinisterhorrorcompany
Twitter @SinisterHC

SINISTERHORRORCOMPANY.COM